The Return of the Pinfire Lady

Lady Abigail Penraven returns to her native England to deal with family matters, but a visit to a London gunsmith to repair her trusty Pinfire revolver leads to the kidnapping of her Ute Indian friend Minny. The subsequent gunplay results in Abbie killing a thug who, unbeknown to her, was involved in a conspiracy to thwart the USA's purchase of Alaska.

Abbie returns to the USA in a new role as a British Government agent working with the US, but finds herself caught up in treachery, intrigue and skulduggery, and has to draw on all the skills that first led her to become known as the 'Pinfire Lady'.

The Return of the Pinfire Lady

P.J. Gallagher

A Black Horse Western

ROBERT HALE

Typeset by
Derek Doyle & Associates, Shaw Heath
Printed and bound in Great Britain by
4Bind Ltd, Stevenage, SG1 2XT

Dedicated to my sister Amelia and to my late brother Harold,
who is sorely missed.

CHAPTER 1

Blam! Blam! Boom! The noise of two pistol shots followed by the deep sound of a shotgun being discharged echoed and reverberated around the confines of the showroom of Caleb Lawden's gun shop.

Tendrils of thick grey smoke slowly spiralled towards the ceiling as Abigail Penraven slowly rose from the gun-fighting crouch she had automatically assumed when faced with a killer intent on mayhem. Her Pinfire revolver, still grasped firmly in both hands, remained aimed at the bloody, huddled remains of what had been the vulpine-faced London character known to the underworld as Jimmy the Wolf.

Thoughts flashed through Abbie's mind as she attempted to reconcile the result of a simple visit to England to wind up family affairs with the vicious attempt to shoot both her and Minny, her loyal Ute companion. The two women had been great friends for years, ever since each had saved the other's life during the affair known in Colorado's history as the 'Comanchero Raid'.

When Lady Penraven had to return to England from her home in Colorado to attend to the estate of her only relative, her late Uncle George, she had asked Minny if she would like to accompany her. Minny up to that time had never travelled anywhere apart from an expedition down into Texas. She was curious about the strange land from which her friend Abbie came, and somewhat apprehensively had agreed to the arrangement.

Minny, with her glossy black hair, smooth brown complexion, and smiling brown eyes yet solemn visage, had been an instant attraction with quite a number of the young Englishmen with whom they had come in contact. Rumour had it that Minny was a princess of the Ute nation, and neither she nor Abbie attempted to correct this impression.

It had been a most interesting visit, especially for Minny, who had stared with awe as together they toured the Tower of London and Westminster Abbey, and giggled as they experienced the strange way that sounds travel in the Whispering Gallery of St Paul's Cathedral. Minny, with her complete trust in Abbie's judgment, had come to accept all the strange experiences that had come her way since leaving Colorado: the sea voyage, which she had stoically endured; the train journeys which she had loved; the life in hotels both in the United States and in this London, where so many people rushed hither and thither, while speaking in a strange form of English very different to that used by Abbie.

Having settled Uncle George's estate, there was one more thing Abbie had wanted to do before leaving London. Her Pinfire revolver had served her well in the years since she had first received it as a gift from her late uncle, but it required servicing, and, as a Tipping and Lawden product, she figured that, since they were in

London where the gunsmiths had a store, she might as well have it repaired before leaving the city.

Following directions, she and Minny together had located the shop, and pushing open the door, had stepped inside the dimly lit salesroom that ran from one side of the store to the other. They had noted a number of assorted long guns racked vertically on the wall facing the entrance, and a glass case on the counter containing several handguns, among which nestled two Sharps four-barrelled derringers.

Her entry, and that of her silent companion following closely at her heels, had prompted the ringing of a bell mounted on the lintel above the door, and as she approached the counter, a small man garbed in oil- and grease-spattered working clothes had stepped out from an inner room and stood smiling, yet more than a little curious as to the two women confronting him. The one facing him was an extremely handsome young woman, he hazarded still in her twenties. The auburn hair, crowned by a little red hat, was unfashionably bobbed short, and the clear, sun-kissed features showed no sign of artificial adornment. The floor-length travelling suit of expensive-looking grey velvet was curious only because she obviously scorned to wear the ridiculous, crinoline-caged attire considered de rigueur by the leaders of fashion. Her solemn companion with straight black hair was even more modestly dressed, but this was offset by the double-stranded necklace she wore, which, if his old eyes did not betray him, was made from a number of claws and teeth of some large animal not to be found in the United Kingdom. They had indeed seemed a strange pair of customers in a gunsmiths.

9

'Good morning, ladies! Caleb Lawden at your service! How may I assist you?' he had declared in a pleasant voice that contained more than a trace of his northern upbringing.

Abbie had smiled in reply and introduced herself: 'I am Lady Penraven, and this is my friend and companion Miss Minny Ute. I am wondering if you could repair and refurbish this gun, which I understand was one of your products?' So saying, she had reached into a large travelling bag and produced a long-barrelled Pinfire revolver tucked into a home-made leather holster. Handing the weapon across the counter, she had pointed out that the loading gate was barely secured since it was badly cracked at the hinge, and she had waited silently whilst Mr Lawden examined the pistol, pursing his lips and tut-tutting as he turned the piece over and over in his hands.

He had observed that the gun had had hard treatment from the time that it had left their showroom. The chequered grips of the handle were worn almost smooth, as were the serrations of the thumb-piece of the hammer, whilst the barrel close to the muzzle was polished bright, indicating that the piece had been often drawn from the leather holster lying on the counter.

'Well, m'lady, we didn't make many of these Pinfire revolvers, they never did become popular in England, but we may have some parts still in stock. Just one moment.' He rummaged around in a nest of small drawers, opening and shutting them one after another, all the while muttering under his breath 'Gate! Part 14! Gate! Part 14!'

Suddenly his explorations had been violently and loudly interrupted as the shop door was thrown open to permit the entry of a large, vulgar creature wearing a loud checked coat and brown moleskin trousers.

'Lawden, yer miserable blackguard! Where's me shooter? Yer promised to 'ave it done firs' thing s'mornin', an' 'ere yer are fiddling abaht wi've a couple of dollies instead've gettin' on wiv my job!' – so saying, he had marched forward, pushing Minny to one side to pound his right fist on the counter top, demanding that Caleb Lawden drop all other work and attend to his needs.

William Sykes, of the loud voice and even louder apparel, and named after his late unlamented grandfather, had made a large number of mistakes in his lifetime of three decades, two of them in the previous minute. As his arm came down to hit the counter there was the flash of a large object, and he had found his right sleeve pinned firmly to the woodwork by a Bowie knife in the hands of the brown-faced girl he had dismissed but moments before. Simultaneously he had found the muzzle of a small revolver pressed against his right temple and the action cocked by the lady in the grey habit, who, without raising her voice, had addressed him in a commanding voice:

'Don't venture to move a muscle or even blink an eyelid, you uncouth specimen. My companion is an expert with her little knife and she'll remove your manhood in a split second, if I have not already relieved you of whatever limited brains you may possess in your miserable skull.'

The tableau had remained frozen for what seemed to be an eternity, with both Lawden and Sykes rigid and with mouths agape, the former with surprise and the latter with both shock and terror at the thought that either of the lady's threats should be put into practice. Finally Sykes had broken the silence, visibly gulping and muttering an

11

abject apology to the two women – though inwardly he was seething with anger and embarrassment, thankful only for the fact that none of his associates had observed his predicament.

In response to his excuses for his loutish behaviour, Abbie Penraven had nodded to her Indian friend, who wordlessly had retrieved her gleaming knife, though she continued to cradle it prominently in her arms as her lady-ship uncocked the little 31-calibre Colt and slipped it into a pocket. Without a word Sykes had slunk from the shop, while silently he swore revenge for the indignities he had experienced.

Caleb Lawden, after apologizing for the behaviour of the ill-mannered intruder, had proceeded to strip down Abbie's Pinfire revolver; he had then cleaned and hand polished each part, and had reassembled it, not forgetting to replace the damaged loading gate with a new piece obtained from his stock in the nest of drawers.

Whilst the gunsmith was thus engaged, Abbie had given him a brief account of her history and the part played by the gun on which he was working. She told how, after being the sole survivor of a wagon train massacre, she had encountered an old mountain man who had taught her survival skills and much lore of the west. She had already been familiar with guns, but he had helped her hone her skills at drawing and repeatedly hitting targets. Abbie admitted that, through no fault of her own, she had been forced into gunfights from which, fortunately, she had emerged the winner.

This was her first visit to England since travelling to the United States in 1858, and had come about because of the death of her only relative, her father's brother George. As the sole executor she had reluctantly made the journey, and was eager to wind up her deceased uncle's affairs and wanted to return to her home in Colorado.

Caleb Lawden listened to her account with a small smile on his lips. He had heard many tall stories from customers over the years, but this tale from the polite lady in front of him took the biscuit. She had undoubtedly experienced some hardships in her life, but gunfights. . . ?

He finished his task of checking her Pinfire, and placing it on the counter, reached down to a lower shelf and placed a box of 12mm cartridges next to the pistol. 'The cartridges are a little gift, m'lady. The work on the gun would be covered by a half sovereign. If that's all right with you, m'lady.'

Abbie had indicated that she was perfectly satisfied, and picking up her pistol had added a comment that sounded odd to the English gunsmith: 'Billy Curtis always maintained that an unloaded pistol is no better than a hammer. So I had better rectify the situation with regard to my pistol' – and opening the replaced loading gate, she had rapidly and expertly loaded five rounds.

It was providential that she did so, because at that very moment a cloaked figure with a dirty blue muffler half concealing his features had entered the shop and started to produce an ugly bell-mouthed blunderbuss from within the folds of his clothing. As he did so he had fortunately announced his intentions in a loud and grating voice: ''Ere's a little present! Complements of Mr William Sykes! Share this between yer!'

Abbie, her senses continually sharpened during the

years on the western frontier, had been aware of danger the moment the door had opened, and as the stranger brought out his weapon, she had therefore immediately taken action: dropping down on one knee, she had grasped her pistol in the familiar grip of left hand on the trigger guard ahead of the cylinder, simultaneously cocking the piece with her left thumb as her right forefinger nestled round the trigger.

Jimmy the Wolf realized too late that he had made a fatal error in taking on this latest assignment: flames had blossomed from the woman in front, and he received two violent, hammer-like blows in the chest, which knocked him back in the doorway. His last conscious thought as his eyes clouded over was to curse Sykes who had prevailed upon him to do the job. The blunderbuss, still pointed downwards, had bellowed as Jimmy's dying finger squeezed the trigger and lead shot buried itself in the wooden floor. Acrid gun smoke hung in the air, and Caleb Lawden had breathed an audible whisper of 'Blimey!'

Abbie, with a skill born of long practice, punched out the two expended cartridge cases and reloaded the empty chambers; she then slid the pistol into its holster and replaced the weapon and the box of 12mm cartridges in the grip she was carrying.

While she was thus engaged, two 'peelers' appeared, summoned by a police whistle; they took down information from all concerned, and removed Jimmy's corpse, which was leaking badly. Next to appear was Police Inspector Gordon, an astute gentleman with a clipped military moustache; after listening to, and examining all the evidence, he declared that Lady Penraven had acted in self-defence against an unprovoked assault, and that no charges would be laid in the matter. All parties were therefore free to go about their lawful business.

Abbie and Minny departed the gunsmiths and, travelling in a cab summoned by Inspector Gordon, returned to Brown's hotel where they had been staying for the last three weeks while Abbie wound up the affairs of her departed Uncle George. Attending to the servicing of her Pinfire pistol had been one of the last tasks she had wanted to perform before returning to Colorado.

Minny kept most of her thoughts to herself, but had come to realize that this London as proving to be just as dangerous as Colorado. She had enjoyed her experiences with Abbie, but now she was more than ready to return to her people. However, first she thought she would like to buy a little gift for her mother – maybe a nice string of beads, the ones that the White Eyes called pearls. She had money, Abbie had seen to that, and she had already made various small purchases; so she approached her friend and stated her intention of going to the jewellers just down the street from the hotel.

'That's a great idea, Minny! I'll get my hat and coat and come with you.'

Minny raised one brown hand, 'No, Abbie! You stay here and rest, this Minny can do by herself.'

Reluctantly Abbie agreed to Minny's suggestion and the Ute girl departed, while Abbie continued her self-appointed task of sorting her uncle's papers into some resemblance of order.

CHAPTER 2

The long summer day passed and still Minny had not returned from her shopping expedition. The sun was sinking towards the western horizon and Abbie was beginning to consider that Minny's absence was becoming overlong. As this thought passed through her mind there was a light knock at the hotel door and a folded note appeared on the polished floor. Abbie ran forward and threw open the door just in time to see a shadowy figure leap down the stairway and disappear from sight. Returning to their room she picked up the pencilled note written on brown paper, obviously torn from a roll of commercial material, and read: 'If yer wants to see yer little brown frend alive, com by yeself to the Black Cat, Dyott St. 10 o'clock t'night.' The note was signed 'W. Sykes'.

Abbie threw herself into an armchair to consider the problem. Obviously this was a reaction to the episode that morning in Lawden's gun shop – though probably less as a result of the demise of Jimmy the Wolf, than the self-inflicted embarrassment Sykes had felt as a result of his treatment at the hands of the two women. Should she go to the police? Possibly. But the note had stressed that she go alone to this Black Cat, wherever it was located. If she arrived with a group of 'peelers' there was no telling what would happen!

Her reverie was interrupted by the entry of Mollie, the little chambermaid assigned to the room. Noting that the room was occupied, she started to withdraw, but Abbie motioned to her to stay while she stared at the girl critically. Mollie was probably about sixteen years of age, but looked much younger. She had a pinched little face with lank blonde hair, and an air of being perpetually terrified of making a mistake. Her undernourished body was wrapped in a gown obviously designed for an older and certainly plumper woman – probably the original owner of the worn-out shoes in which she shuffled along.

'Mollie dear, you are a London-bred girl are you not? Have you ever heard of the Black Cat, a public house on Dyott Street, wherever that might be?'

'Dunno anyfink about Black Cat pubs, milady, but I's 'eard of Dyott Street. That's got a bad nyme. It's right in the middle of the Rookery, St Giles Rookery, that is. It's got an orful what jer call it . . . reputation. Me dad would kill me if I ever went there!'

Abbie suggested that perhaps Mollie draw a map showing how to get to Dyott Street, but well nigh terrified, the girl shook her head violently. Finally she was persuaded to go and fetch Bobby Wright, a boot-black in the hotel. Apparently the two of them had what they described as 'an understanding', and Bobby knew the area far more than she did.

Mollie went and reappeared with Bobby Wright in tow, and introduced him to Abbie. She saw in him the male example of the underfed and under-paid Londoner. Bobby was possibly the same age or a little older than his girlfriend, and his gamin features might have been quite presentable if it were not for the mass of adolescent pimples that marred his visage. Like Mollie, he was clad in 'hand-me-down' clothing and a pair of Bluchers that had long ago seen better days. But despite his unprepossessing appearance, Bobby showed intelligence and rapidly sketched out a map on notepaper showing the route Abbie would have to take to get to the Black Cat.

'Mind you, milady, that's an 'orrible place ter visit. A body would want half a dozen troopers to go there, an' no mistake!'

Master Bobby declined Abbie's invitation to accompany her to the Black Cat, and after generous remuneration he and Mollie departed. Thirty minutes later Abbie also left, after a lightning change of her attire. Now clad in her old buckskin shirt, booted, and wearing her soft leather pants, with her pistol holstered on her left hip, balanced by her razor-sharp Bowie knife on the right side, all concealed by an ankle-length travelling cloak, Abbie felt ready for come what may.

Hailing a cab, she instructed the driver to proceed along Oxford Street towards the church of St Giles, at which point she alighted, paid her fare, and ventured into the noisome warren of streets nicknamed the Rookery, or Seven Dials. Ancient buildings with broken windows, their sagging walls shored up with huge baulks of timber, threatened to collapse into the street on either side. From these same buildings came an indescribable babble of voices, yelling, screaming, singing and cursing as the inhabitants lived out their lives amid conditions truly identical to those Abbie had seen in Hogarth's illustrations of these self-same quarters.

She picked her way along ordure-littered streets, stepping over heaps of rubbish, and here and there a dead cat or dog, and moving more cautiously around the recumbent figures of both sexes lying asleep in a drunken stupor. Unseen figures accosted her from shadowy doorways, and she clutched tightly at the 31 Colt pistol in her right cloak pocket, while her left hand held a scarf across her face, partly for concealment but also in an attempt to reduce the vile odours with which her nostrils were assailed.

Eventually her perilous journey was rewarded, as ahead she noted a large sign, depicting a big ugly cat spitting defiance at the world, above a narrow entry from which came the sounds of drunken singing. Keeping on the opposite side of the street, Abbie shuffled past the Black Cat with head down, whilst risking a quick glance to her left as she passed the entry. Yes! Her suspicions were correct. Two men were standing there, watching closely all who approached the doorway. Fortunately they ignored the old figure limping along across the way.

In passing, Abbie had noticed a narrow alleyway between the Black Cat and the neighbouring building, and reaching a point where the curve of the street obscured her from the two watchers, she crossed over and retraced her steps, carefully sidling along until, reaching the alley, she slipped silently down it.

She had surmised that, like most hostelries big and small both in England and in the United States the Black Cat probably had a rear yard where empty bottles and kegs, along with all manner of rubbish and discarded objects, were stored or thrown away. She was correct: there was such a yard, merely fenced with rotting palings with gaps permitting her to gain entry and cross over to where an open door gave entry to what was, apparently, from the odours coming forth, a kitchen.

Abbie took off her cloak and replaced it by merely draping the material across her shoulders. Thus she thought that in a showdown she could throw the garment off leaving her gun and knife hands free.

Having organized her equipment the best way she knew how, she crept into the empty kitchen and thence into a narrow hallway. One archway led into a large taproom, from which came the sounds of clinking glasses and drunken singing. Further down the hall was a stairway leading to an upper floor. The whole of the interior of the building was as dilapidated as the exterior, with rotted wallpaper hanging from the walls, and broken stair-rails supporting a balustrade that had seen better days. The hallway was but ill lit by a single oil lamp in a wall sconce.

Abbie stood at the foot of the stairs, and just as she was about to creep up them, a door opened on the landing above and she quickly moved and crouched in the space under the staircase. Above, a voice that she recognized ordered roughly: 'You git down them there stairs, Jem, an' keep yer peepers peeled fer my guest. I've got a nice little surprise for her!'

Jem muttered something inaudible and stomped down

the stairs, and from his subsequent movements made himself comfortable on the bottom tread as the door on the landing closed noisily.

Abbie waited a few moments and then crept towards Jem, grasping her pistol by the barrel. At the last second Jem turned, but before he could do anything, the butt of the Pinfire crashed down on his temple and he slumped forward; she lowered his unconscious body to the floor.

There was no sound from above, indicating that her activity had gone unnoticed. Abbie holstered her pistol and silently crept up the stairs, keeping close to the wall and away from the unsteady balustrade. She moved cautiously forward to the closed door, which had a light shining at its base. A murmur of voices came from within, and she strained to hear, both to determine who was in the room, and to try to understand the nature of the threat facing her.

Sykes, the crude character she had already encountered, was holding forth: 'An' when we get hold of the other vixen . . .' (obviously referring to Abbie herself) '. . . I've got a little treat in store for her and her mate. A little sea voyage to Algiers, or maybe Tunis. There's houses there which are always looking for fresh girls, and those two will fetch a pretty penny.'

Abbie shivered at the grim fate this scoundrel planned for her and Minny, and seeing a well placed knot-hole, peered into the room. Light was provided by an oil lamp hanging from the ceiling. In the centre of the room was a table, around which lolled Sykes and two of his henchmen, while in the far right corner was a gagged Minny, sitting on the floor with her hands bound behind her back.

Placing herself square in front of the opening, Abbie took a deep breath, paused momentarily, and then, throwing the door wide open, stepped inside and took a pace sideways with her back against the wall.

'Good evening, Mr Sykes! I understand that you wished to see me!' – so saying she allowed the cloak to slip from her shoulders, revealing her frontier garb of dress and her weapons of holstered pistol with another small one thrust through a waist belt, and a wicked-looking Bowie hanging on her right hip.

The individual so addressed leapt to his feet, followed by his two henchmen. 'Curse you, woman! How did you get in here? Get her, lads!' So saying he moved towards Abbie, dragging an Adams revolver from a pocket as he did so.

Raising her left hand and using her wagon-train leader's voice, Abbie cried: 'Stop! Don't move another step or it will be the worse for you!'

Her command had no effect, so Abbie went into gun-fighting mode. She crouched as her right hand swept across to draw her 12mm pistol, while at the same time her left hand grasped the piece forward of the trigger guard as the right thumb cocked the hammer.

Too late Sykes realized that the small attractive woman with the lardy-da accent was not fooling: her pistol spoke long before he was ready to fire. Then she fired yet again, and he crashed backwards on to the floor as his life slipped away.

One of his associates did manage to actually get his weapon, a double-barrelled percussion pistol, into action and the ball plucked at Abbie's buckskin shirt. She returned the fire, and before his pistol could speak again he was propelled backwards with a smashed shoulder, his pistol dropping from his useless hand. The third member of the unsavoury trio, suddenly realizing that life was sweet, stood there with his hands high, pleading for his life.

Reloading, Abbie swiftly crossed the room, tore off Minny's gag, and with several strokes of her Bowie knife secured the Ute's release. Shakily Minny rose to her feet and clung to Abbie, 'Oh, Abbie! I am so happy to see you! These men, they say bad things happen to us and. . . .'

Abbie interrupted her excited discourse: 'Later Minny! First we have to get out of here!'

Even as she said these last words the remaining villain, still with his arms raised, had been slinking slowly towards the door, and while their attention was diverted by their joyful reunion, darted through the opening and fled down the stairs yelling 'Help! Help! Murder!'

From the noise that erupted from the lower level it was apparent that the cry for help had received immediate attention as patrons arrived from the taproom, followed by the outer guards.

Hearing the commotion below, Abbie realized that retreat by way of the stairs was out of the question, and that equally, the two of them were badly outnumbered if they chose to make a stand on the landing. Shutting the door to the room in which Minny had been imprisoned, and calling upon her companion to help, Abbie dragged the table over and jammed it under the door handle.

There was a small window, its grimy dirt-encrusted glass remarkably intact, which looked out over the slate roof of the kitchen by which Abbie had entered the Black Cat, a window that had been nailed shut in the distant past. There was no time to lose, so she picked up a chair and smashed the glass and the rotten wood securing the panes in place, sweeping her cumbersome tool back and forth to remove as many shards as she could. Picking up her grey cloak, she draped it over the now gaping window-hole and motioned to Minny: 'Come on Minny! Out you go!' – and Minny, encumbered by her long skirt, did as instructed: gathering up her dress in a most unladylike fashion, she squeezed through the opening and dropped down on to the roof below.

Abbie followed, pausing whilst astride the window to fire one shot through the closed door at the knot of men now hammering at the far side. There was a single cry and then a short silence, during which time she joined Minny: the two of them crept across the slates, and by a convenient drainpipe, climbed down to the rubbish-strewn inn yard.

Holding hands, the two girls crept down the alley towards Dyott Street, only to be halted by large numbers of men spilling forth from the Black Cat like bees out of an overturned bee-hive, all adding to the hue and cry. Abbie halted in dismay as the chance of escape down Dyott Street rapidly disappeared. But at that very moment fate appeared to intervene to furnish the means of escape for the two fugitives.

Abbie felt a tap on her arm, and in the darkness of the alley looked down to see a boy staring up at her.

'Excuse me, miss,' he said politely, 'I don't think you're going to get out that way. If you trust me I can guide you and get us all clear of the Rookery.'

Abbie nodded a speechless assent, and their new-found friend led them down the alley and across the next street, and then by alleys, back yards, through tumbledown buildings and by a myriad other ways, they made their way through the warren of the Rookery until they reached Oxford Street.

Whilst travelling their young guide was full of information about the area and himself. No, he didn't live in the Rookery but was actually being truant from school. Well, not really truant since the scholars had been given a half-day holiday, but absent without permission. And, yes, he would probably get a wigging when he returned. It seemed that he was fascinated by all the various types of people to be found in the great metropolis, and he wished to learn all that he could regarding their speech, slang, style of dress, occupations and living habits. 'It's a lot more interesting than the stuff they cram down us at school, miss!'

The strange boy had one more piece of advice before they hailed a cab: he suggested that Minny loan Abbie her travelling coat to conceal the latter's garb and weapons.

'Now I must be off, miss – good luck!' and he stuck out his hand. Abbie responded warmly, shaking hands vigorously. 'Thank you! Thank you! And to whom do we owe our good fortune?'

The boy literally wriggled in embarrassment as he replied; 'It's nothing, Miss! Holmes is the name, Sherlock Holmes!' So saying he ran off into the darkness.

Safe in the hotel once more, Minny described how, having made her purchase, she had been approached by a

25

stranger who told her that Abbie had had an accident and needed assistance. Of course Minny had responded to this appeal and had been bundled into a cab – but here a sack was thrown over her head, and finally she ended up in the room where Abbie had found her. And on that note the two exhausted girls prepared for bed.

CHAPTER 3

The following morning after packing and completing their individual toilette they took breakfast and returned to their bedroom. Shortly after there was a knock at the door, and to their surprise and dismay they found they had visitors in the form of Inspector Gordon, a police constable, a grey-haired well dressed gentleman who studied them gravely, followed by a younger man, well built, bronzed, and fashionably dressed as a North American gentleman.

Indicating that the constable should remain in the corridor, the other three entered the room and closed the door. Inspector Gordon motioned the women to be seated, and he and his silent companions stood, studying them gravely. Finally, the inspector spoke in measured tones with just a trace of his Scottish background: 'Last night at about ten or eleven o'clock there was a very serious disturbance in the parish of St Giles, more precisely in the area known locally as the Rookery. In the general disturbance shots were fired, resulting in the death of one William Sykes, a reputed housebreaker and recorded criminal. I might add that a number of 12mm Pinfire cases were found at the scene!' He paused, looked at Abbie, and queried: 'Lady Penraven! Would you know anything about this matter?'

Abbie regarded the smartly uniformed official gravely for a moment, and then described in great detail the whole sorry story of Minny's kidnapping and her own reaction, leaving out only the aid rendered by the strange boy. She saw no reason why he should get into trouble on their account.

The grey-haired gentleman, austerely dressed in black morning coat with silk cravat and pale grey trousers who, hitherto, had remained silent now spoke, 'Lady Penraven. You have been living in the United States for these past several years?' Abbie nodded. 'Are you then an American citizen?' Abbie shook her head.

When she first arrived in the States she had had no intention of remaining. Then, as the years passed and having a ranch, mining interests, bandits and other issues to contend with, the issue of citizenship had not arisen. That is until 1861, when the whole country had become engulfed in the Civil War which had pitted neighbour against neighbour, and Abbie found herself plumb centre in the conflict. Having friends from both North and South she had been determined to remain neutral during the conflict and remained that way until the war ended in the present year, that is, 1865.

'So we may assume that you are still a loyal subject of her most gracious majesty, Queen Victoria?'

Abbie inclined her head in slow agreement, wondering where this discussion was leading.

'Now, ma'am, you must realize that if this shooting were taken to court, and despite the mitigating circumstances you were found to be guilty, it would mean imprisonment, which is not a pleasant prospect. However, her Majesty's government does not want this problem to be resolved in that manner. It would certainly create more problems with the American Federal Government, and we already have sufficient, what with the negotiations regarding reparations over the activities of the Alabama.' (He referred, of course, to the exploits of the Liverpool-built Confederate ocean raider.)

'This is what the Prime Minister proposes. The Rookery affair will be hushed up, lost in the files as it were, in return for which you will undertake to become an agent for the British government whilst residing in the western United States. At this point I can assure you that you will never be employed in any activity which may cause harm to your country of residence.' He turned to his younger companion: 'I think that you have the floor, sir.'

The other civilian rose and addressed Abbie: 'Lady Penraven. My name is Roger Gotwald and I work for the United States Government.' He extracted a card from a leather wallet, and handed it to her.

Abbie took the proffered card and examined it curiously: it was a heavily embossed pasteboard bearing the words 'Office of the United States of America', and signed by a man known to millions of his countrymen. On the reverse side was a note introducing Roger F. Gotwald, signed by the Secretary of State, William H. Seward.

'I have worked for Mr Seward for a number of years, and first of all I would like to stress that my government is not after you in any way, but rather, we feel that with your unusual skills you may be able to assist not only the country of your residence, but also the country of your birth.

'It would appear that somehow you have become involved in an international conspiracy.' He saw that Abbie was going to raise questions, and putting up a hand, he hurriedly continued: 'You may not be aware that, currently, my government is negotiating with representatives of the Tsarist Imperial government of Russia to purchase Alaska. Count Nikolai Stroganoff is the leader of a movement seeking to thwart the purchase. He and his companions want the inhabitants of Alaska to declare independence from Russia and be recognized as a separate country. An American, Hiram P. Markover, a New York banker, and a Britisher, Sir Bertram Wallace, are also deeply involved in this conspiracy. We believe that Wallace has some notion of severing part of British Columbia away from Canada and making it part of Alaskiana.

'Now, this is where you enter the picture, Lady Penraven. One of Wallace's chief henchmen in London was a certain William Sykes, now indisposed, shall we say! They apparently believe that you have discovered their plans and that therefore you have become an enemy who must be eliminated. We, that is both of our governments, are hoping that you will accept the challenge and join us in destroying Stroganoff and his companions.'

Abbie was silent for a few moments as she considered the options; then, finally looking up, she smiled, nodding her head slowly as she answered his plea by indicating that she would do whatever she could to assist both governments in resolving the Alaska situation. With that understanding the meeting ended and the officials left.

Abbie turned and smiled at Minny, who sat there totally bewildered by the conversation: 'Don't worry, Minny! Everything is going to be all right. I'll tell you one day.'

And thus henceforth Abbie was an agent of the British Government, but also in the service of the United States.

CHAPTER 4

As the stagecoach drew closer to Julesburg, Abbie looked back over the journey, which had taken the pair of them several weeks. The voyage across the Atlantic was uneventful, apart from one incident aboard ship where a block had fallen to the deck, missing her by inches – but it could very well have been an accident. Equally uneventful was their arrival in New York, where the steerage passengers with their pitiful bundles waited for hours to be permitted ashore, whilst the first class passengers, including Abbie and Minny, were treated like royalty, and escorted down the gangplank to the waiting cab rank.

Whilst still in England, Abbie had realized that a number of her sex were rebelling against the accepted restrictions of dress, with their tightly laced apparel, monstrous crinolines and absurd bustles. Ever a maverick, Abbie had adopted the attire chosen by women in intellectual circles, of fairly plain, loose-fitting clothes which had come into vogue earlier in the decade. For one thing this type of dress was far more practical for travelling.

Minny, of course, was eager to follow Abbie's lead in this matter.

Thus attired, they journeyed westward by train or, as quaintly described by their fellow travellers, riding on the 'steam cars'. Traversing each state seemed to bring forth its own excitement. Since the period was less than twelve months after the surrender of Lee's army at Appomattox, the whole country was still in turmoil and unstable. Crime was rife. Huge numbers of Union soldiers discharged from the army were trying to return to their homes, as were thousands of released Confederates. And many of these men, after four years of war where the notion of private property depended on who was winning, constituted a danger to the general public. To these were added vast numbers of black folk now released from bondage in the South, yet rejected in the northern states as a threat to the livelihood of industrial workers. And finally there was a steady increase in the gangs of young embittered men who refused to accept that the South had lost the war, and who maintained a guerrilla campaign of bank robbery in various parts of the country.

Approaching Seymour, Indiana, a small community nestling in the foothills just north of the mighty Ohio River, their train was held up by a band of mounted, heavily armed riders intent on robbing the passengers of all they possessed. Abbie, who was carrying her Pinfire pistol in a carpet bag, had absolutely no intention of surrendering anything to the pair of dishevelled ruffians who entered their particular coach bellowing cries of, 'Hands up, an' keep 'em up!' to the startled inmates.

Swiftly her right hand entered the bag and emerged

with the pistol, and cocking the hammer, she chanced a snap shot at the burly figure flourishing a .32 calibre Smith and Wesson in his grubby paw. Her gun bellowed, and the 12mm lead bullet hit the bandit in the right arm just above the wrist: it ripped upwards, coming out at the elbow and then embedding itself in the door.

The would-be robber screamed, and clutching his wounded arm, screamed again as his pistol dropped to the floor. His associate stood aghast for a second, and then turned and made a hasty exit, leaving the wounded one to face the consequences. The whole gang then fled from the scene. At Seymour the wounded train robber was handed over to the authorities, declaring that he was a friend of the Reno brothers, known to be committing crimes all over southern Indiana.

Abbie gave a brief statement. She was commended for her swift action, and she and Minny continued on their journey. (Two years later Abbie read how members of the Reno gang had been taken out of jail and lynched by vigilantes.)

Abbie made enquiries at a number of rail and coach lines to try and determine which would be the fastest mode of travel to take when returning to her home near Colorado City, given the progress being made regarding land travel. Should she choose the long but familiar route of the Santa Fe Trail, or possibly the Overland Trail? The latter started from Atchison, Missouri, and took a far more northern route across Kansas, dipping down to Julesburg, Colorado, before heading north-west and linking up with the Oregon Trail at Fort Bridger. The stagecoach journey from Atchison to Julesburg was estimated to be about 460 miles, which, barring accidents or other mishaps, would take no more than four days, since the coach travelled both day and night.

After due consideration and consultations with Minny, they decided to take the coach to Julesburg, buy horses there and travel south, stopping for a couple of days to visit friends in Denver. That city, they were told, was a far cry from the frontier settlement Abbie recalled visiting some time before the war. Gold had been discovered in 1858 at a settlement known as Montana City, which became known as Auraria in 1859, then Denver, and eventually in 1867 it became the territorial capital. But that was in the future.

Whilst seated in a frontier hotel reading a newspaper and awaiting the arrival of the coach that was to take them westward, Abbie was interrupted by a shadow that was cast over the paper – looking up, she found a tall, sturdily built frontiersman looking down and regarding her quizzically. He was dressed in a fringed buckskin shirt with cavalry pants tucked into long boots.

'Pardon me, ma'am, for interrupting your reading, but would you be the one people call the Pinfire Lady?'

Irritated that her carefully concealed *nom de guerre* was thus so readily bandied about, Abbie acknowledged tartly that that indeed was what some folks called her – and inquired sharply: 'And you might be?' Aware that he had made a social blunder, the stranger hurriedly removed his slouch hat, apologizing as he did so. 'Sorry Ma'am! I was out of turn, I guess. My name is Hickok, James Butler Hickok, but folks call me Wild Bill. Not quite sure why,' he declared a trifle ruefully.

Abbie smiled knowingly, and observed: 'Are you the gentleman who reportedly had a duel with one David Tutt in Springfield, Missouri, last year and put a bullet into his heart at seventy-five yards? A remarkable achievement perhaps – but surely you didn't wish to discuss your prowess with a pistol?'

She gestured towards the pair of muzzle-loading Colts prominently displayed in a strange reverse position, and then motioned for Wild Bill to take a seat on the couch beside her, taking note as she did so of his seemingly flamboyant appearance of shoulder-length hair and long, drooping moustache.

Hickok seated himself and explained that, although he was currently a deputy marshal at Fort Riley, he was also engaged as an army scout for Colonel Custer, the officer commanding the 7th Cavalry. In such capacity he had noted with concern increased Indian activity all along the route used by the overland stagecoach, and had cautioned the various stage managers, although these had tended to belittle his well meant warnings. Therefore, receiving word that the Pinfire Lady was in town and intending to ride the stage to Julesburg, he thought perhaps she would take heed of what he had to say.

'I believe, ma'am, that in the past you have made yourself a reputation for taking decisive action as the situation desired, and I merely thought that you might wish to be forewarned about possible trouble along the trail.'

Abbie thanked Wild Bill, and after a brief discussion regarding the merits of Pinfire cartridges versus a brace of muzzle-loading revolvers, excused herself. Then she and the ever watchful Minny left to make a rapid change into their frontier garb, deciding that if there was any possibility of turmoil it would be wise to dress for the occasion, as it were.

CHAPTER 5

Thus attired with firearms concealed by their travelling cloaks, they, together with their luggage, left the hotel, summoned by the arrival of the Concord coach with its six mettlesome horses straining at the traces and eager to commence their run.

The passengers introduced themselves to each other as they entered the coach, most being fully aware of the need for pleasant companionship on the long journey. Abbie and Minny followed suit and thus became familiar with their fellow travellers: Rachel Smith, a rather plain twenty-three-year-old on her way to a teaching job in Denver; Ed Colvill, 'Call me Slick Ed', a professional gambler; Isaiah Lowe, a dour, tight-lipped merchant; a nattily dressed young man sporting a brace of pistols who intimated that he was quick on the draw and called himself 'Flash Harry'; James Crowe, a salesman, who boasted that he travelled in lady's underwear; and finally two soldiers, a Captain Wainwright and a Sergeant Johnson, who both seemed to be travelling on detached service. As well as the passengers inside the coach were two buckskin-clad outriders; the driver, or to give him his full title, the conductor, called Ben by name, but commonly nicknamed Jehu, after the biblical figure; and Buck, the guard who was bearing a shotgun.

In true frontier fashion Ben, the driver, lashed at the team and the stagecoach left Atchison at a gallop, to the cheers of passers-by on the boardwalks; but soon they were headed westward at a steady five miles an hour, with the body of the coach bucking and swaying in its stout leather suspension over the undulating prairie which, with its monotonous terrain, reminded Abbie of her westward trek with Billy Curtis. Most of the passengers settled as best they could and started up desultory conversations with each other. Considerable interest was displayed by some of the passengers upon learning that Abbie was an Englishwoman, though she revealed nothing of her past.

It wasn't long, however, before some of the travellers began displaying more dubious aspects of their characters. James Crowe, the salesman, opened a carpet bag on his lap, and dipping a hand inside, brought forth a cloth. Unfolding it, he held up with both hands a pair of pink silk lady's drawers adorned with lacy trim and tiny embroidered rosettes.

'Look at these, folks! Latest fashion. Straight from Paris where they're all the rage! I'm prepared to. . . .' He got no further with his sales pitch as, with lightning speed, Slick Ed produced a Derringer from his right sleeve and thrust it into Crowe's temple.

'Just put that away in your carpet bag, mister, or I'm likely to blow a hole right through your head! You seem to forget that we have ladies present. Now apologize!'

Trembling, James Crowe did as he was ordered, and an uneasy silence descended on the coach.

Hours passed. Relay stations came into view, lonely outposts in the wilderness, each consisting of a single-storey building solidly created for defence, with windows that could be shuttered during an alarm and a sod roof which reduced the chances of fire. Each had a large corral confining the draft animals that hauled the coaches. The coach would pound into the station yard, the horses were changed and the stagecoach was off again with hardly enough time for the passengers to step down and stretch their legs. A longer halt was made at noon allowing people time to purchase a basic lunch cooked by the station owner's wife and buy a drink, alcoholic or otherwise; a similar stop was made in the early evening for supper.

Darkness fell and the coach thundered through the night, with its weary load of humans attempting to seek a modicum of rest in their swaying, bone-shaking conveyance. There were several regulations by which the company sought to maintain a certain standard of behaviour among their passengers, one of which was the rule that it was not socially acceptable to rest one's head against the shoulder of a fellow sufferer when attempting to sleep. Minny transgressed.

After restlessly falling asleep, the movement of the vehicle caused her to rock from side to side and finally come to rest upon the shoulder of Flash Harry, the would-be gunfighter. That worthy, becoming aware of her presence, stiffened and then gave voice to a grievance which had been bothering him since the journey commenced. 'Get away from me, you stinkin' squaw. It's bad enough having to travel all crammed together like this without having to put up with a lousy Indian sitting on my lap. What's she doing in here anyway? I thought anyone other than white folks had to travel up top!'

In vain poor Minny endeavoured to placate the irate youth, apologizing in clear but broken English. Abbie deliberately refrained from entering the fray, wanting to see how her Ute friend would handle the mishap. Flash Harry continued with his tirade, ignoring Minny's reasoning and, when he paused, it was only to grasp the butts of his two pistols and intimate that, if they were clear of the coach, there would soon be a reckoning.

Minny had had enough. Unseen her hand slipped beneath her cloak and emerged with her razor-sharp Bowie, with which she sliced through Harry's gun-belt, stating firmly, 'Little boys not play with guns! Too easily get hurt. You be good now!' and the panic-stricken young man, only too conscious of the glittering knife waving to and fro a mere two inches in front of his marriage prospects, froze like a stone and, to the amusement of the other passengers, sat there not daring to move a muscle.

As a faint light began to appear along the eastern horizon, heralding the promise of yet another dawn, the stagecoach pulled into the yard of a relay station, and the stiff and weary passengers were informed that they had time to break their fast.

Then occurred the first of a series of mishaps which befell the coach and its passengers. As Ben, the Jehu, made his announcement and prepared to dismount from the driver's box, he somehow slipped and fell to the ground. There was an audible crack as he landed, and the passengers gathered round to see their conductor lying with a broken leg. Ben was carried into the station and the broken limb was straightened and splinted. He looked up at them with a twisted grin on his pain-racked features, 'Well folks, I'm truly sorry of the inconvenience. There's no getting away from the fact that I've created a bit of a fix for ye. With no driver you'll be stuck here until a replacement comes out from Atkinson.'

A babble of voices broke out at his announcement, some declaring that it was imperative that they reach their destination on time, while others made equally impractical suggestions. Abbie and Minny remained silent. Accidents happen. One just has to swing with the event.

A harsh feminine cry cut short the noise around the injured man. 'What's all the row about! Stop all yer squawking! I'll drive yer goddam' coach ter Julesburg, an get yer there afore ole Ben would!' and the people turned to behold a tall, grubby, rawboned woman of indeterminate age, dressed in ragged Levis and a teamster's shirt, regarding them with arms akimbo.

'Martha Jane Cannary is the name, but most folks call me Calamity Jane, or just Calamity! I'm a qualified stagecoach driver' (which she was not) 'and I've just bin takin' a few days holiday with ma friends here.'

Behind her back the owner of the way station was shaking his head vigorously at Calamity's statements, and silently mouthing the word 'No . . .', torn between his desire to get rid of his unwelcome guest, and his desire to solve the dilemma of the disabled stagecoach driver.

The hubbub of argumentative voices broke out afresh and Abbie decided to take command. In a stentorian bellow she roared, 'Quiet all of you!' in her clear, precise English tone, and the group was so surprised to hear their demure fellow passenger hold forth in such a manner that they fell silent.

'Thank you everybody! Now Miss Cannary, perhaps you would elaborate a trifle on your qualifications, which would permit you to take over the driving of our conveyance and look after the welfare of all the passengers?'

Abbie's query brought forth a single response of 'Huh!', together with a look of total incomprehension, which prompted her to re-phrase the question:

'Miss Cannary, is there anyone here who can vouch that you do indeed know how to handle a coach and team of horses?'

'Well, yes, miss. Buck there, the shotgun guard, has seen me. Buck, you git over here and tell these folks what a good driver I am.'

Reluctantly, it seemed, Buck ambled over, wiping beer froth off his tobacco-stained moustache, and reluctantly admitted that Calamity had indeed driven a stagecoach, and no, nobody was killed. After a brief discussion the passengers agreed that rather than be stuck at the way station, Miss Cannary should be hired to replace the injured conductor.

And with that established and new horses ready in the traces, the passengers climbed into the coach to resume their journey – with, however, one exception. Abbie had suggested that for a change she would ride up top next to the driver, while Buck the shotgun guard rode inside. Immediately Minny also stated that she, too, would ride up top among the luggage, and this she did, so as not to be separated from her friend. Overdue, the coach finally got under way, with Abbie keeping a critical eye on Calamity's performance.

CHAPTER 6

As they travelled, Calamity Jane regaled Abbie and Minny with many of her stories, some of which even contained a modicum of truth. She boasted of having been an army scout, a wagon freighter, and having outdrunk most of the men in the west, laughing uproariously at her own jests and describing how, on one occasion, she had decided to become a lady of easy virtue, but the other girls had thrown her out, declaring that she lowered the tone of the house!

Abbie was fully aware that Calamity was attempting to gull her, having decided that she must be a greenhorn; so she merely smiled, and revealed little of her own past as the undulating terrain sped past beneath the wheels of the coach.

So far Calamity was holding her own, controlling the galloping horses with just a flourish of her whip which she wielded expertly. But suddenly the coach shook violently from side to side and Calamity hauled violently on the reins, crying out, 'Whoa! You fleabitten bags of bones!

Whoa, I say!' and brought the conveyance to an abrupt halt.

Abbie, Calamity and Minny dismounted, as did the passengers from inside, all of them demanding to know what had happened. Calamity ignored them, and was running around and inspecting each of the wheels. Quickly she found the cause of their problem, and pointed to the right rear wheel.

'Look at that, will you! The damn wheel nut's gone completely! Must've been running loose ever since we left the last station. How the hell could that've happened?'

Several things then happened instantaneously. A small group of riders was seen approaching at a gallop from the south. Strangely, at the appearance of the horsemen the two military passengers both drew their side-arms and moved to one side to cover their fellow travellers, crying as they did so, 'Hands up all of you or you're dead men!' Typically they ignored the four women, which in the case of Abbie and Minny was a grave mistake. Abbie threw back her cloak, and in one fluid movement drew her Pinfire revolver and fired, giving Captain Wainwright a cyclopic appearance as a 12mm bullet smashed into his forehead. Minny ignored her pistol, choosing instead to toss her Bowie with force at the so-called Sergeant Johnson, who screamed as her razor-sharp knife buried itself in his guts. Rachel Smith fainted.

Abbie took command. 'Quickly you people! Get round to the other side of the coach and either help to drive away these raiders, or keep out of the way while we do the job!' So saying, and dragging the semi-conscious teacher by the arm, she moved around the rear of the coach and fired from under the boot at the oncoming horsemen, who were now shooting wildly.

Nearly all the other people present followed Abbie's example, crouching under the stagecoach or firing over the backs of the team. Slick Ed had rapidly divested Wainwright's corpse of its 1860 model .44 Colt, and Isaiah Lowe had done the same to the dead sergeant. Thus armed they took aim and fired at the would-be robbers, now no more than twenty-five yards distant. Buck the shotgun guard also opened up with a telling blast from his ten-gauge shotgun, and even James Crowe the underwear salesman flourished a puny S and W .22 revolver.

There was just one defector from the group of passengers: waving his arms wildly and running forwards, Flash Harry cried pleadingly, 'I surrender! Don't shoot! I'm not with these folks!' One of the attackers merely laughed at his craven gesticulations, and raising his shotgun he fired, hurling Harry backwards, a lifeless bundle. But his killer had very little time to enjoy his feat as a well-aimed shot from Abbie's revolver drove him from the saddle.

The shooting employed by the stagecoach defenders had reduced the attacking party of eight to three unwounded men, with two others sagging in their saddles. The unknown leader, realizing that the cost of taking the stagecoach was proving too high, evidently ordered a retreat, as the whole party suddenly turned and rode rapidly out of range, then continued to move slowly to the south.

Abbie reloaded and, followed by the others, emerged from her place of concealment. One horse was lying dead in its traces, and another was badly wounded and had to be shot, an unpleasant duty. But with the exception of foolish Harry, not one of the stagecoach crew or passengers was hurt in any way, and all were full of praise for the swift way in which Abbie had reacted to the command to put up her hands.

Grimly, Abbie explained that Ben, the injured Jehu, having been informed by Bill Hickok as to her identity, had told her after his accident that the coach was carrying a large payroll in gold stashed in the forward boot; furthermore he was suspicious of the two 'military' passengers travelling without any papers.

The dead attackers were examined, which revealed that they were wearing remnants of both Federal and Confederate uniforms, indicating that they had probably deserted from both armies. Only one man was given an identity: Calamity saw instantly that one bearded corpse was that of Billy Jones, a member of the large and lawless Missouri family. 'They'll not take Billy's death calmly! They're as mean as cat's dirt, the whole bunch of them, and they'll be seeking revenge!'

The passengers had neither the tools nor the inclination to bury the dead bandits, so the bodies, together with those of their horses, were left on the prairie. Meanwhile their own dead animals were relieved of their harness, and using the other horses, were dragged clear of the trail. Finally, after replacing the wheel nut, the stagecoach set off for the next relay station, though at a slower speed because of the reduced number of horses.

Abbie and Minny had once more chosen to ride up top with Calamity, and the latter was singing a different tune to her boastful display before the attempted hold-up.

'Say Miss Abbie! I've sure got to hand it to you. Where on earth did you learn to shoot like that?'

The questions literally tumbled from her regarding Abbie and her prowess with a pistol: how had she come by the nickname the Pinfire Lady? How many gunfights had she been in, and how many men had she bested? Where did she live in England? And where in Colorado, and did she need a really first class freight bull-wacker?

Abbie skirted round the queries regarding her pistol skills, and meanwhile gave Calamity a very brief outline of life in India and in England, and her life in the western states, tactfully avoiding the subject of possible future employment for one Miss Cannary. Finally, Calamity's interrogation of Abbie ended as the exhausted team hauled the coach into the yard of the next relay station, where they were all bombarded with questions about the attempted hold-up.

While the passengers were enjoying a meal and regaling all within earshot with embellished details of their courageous fight to protect the stagecoach, a small troop of cavalry rode up to the station, accompanied by Bill Hickok. Out on patrol they had found buzzards squabbling over the remains of the horses and men at the scene of the fight, and not knowing the outcome, had ridden post haste westwards to ensure that all was well with the stagecoach.

Wild Bill took Abbie to one side, and from her received an unvarnished account of the affair. Upon learning that one of the dead had been identified by Calamity as Billy Jones, the gunfighter raised one hand bidding Abbie to pause.

'From what you're telling me Abbie, if I may so address you, it was the speed of your reaction to the order to put up your hands that triggered the resistance to those bandits. So when they've had time to think it over, it's you they'll blame for their failure, in addition to the loss of one of their kinfolk.'

Abbie reflected on what Wild Bill had just told her, and shrugging her shoulders, responded ruefully. 'Mr Hickok, you don't paint a very pretty picture regarding the possibility of my living a long, uneventful life, do you? But I do sincerely appreciate the warnings I'm getting from both you and the rest of the people here, and I'll be on my guard.'

Wild Bill nodded as he turned towards the door of the station: 'Jus' remember you're dealing with a bunch of back-shootin' varmints. Always sit with your back to a wall!' he ended on a prophetic note – and was gone out of Abbie's life.

The journey continued. Mile after mile the land rolled away, rising now as the trail entered the foothills of the Rocky Mountains. Relay station after relay station appeared, horses were changed, and at intervals the same kind of boring, uninspired dishes were offered to the weary travellers. It had proved impossible to obtain an alternative Jehu, so Calamity Jane had remained as their driver, and Abbie, less for the frontier woman's company than for the need to maintain a sharp lookout for any sign of the Jones gang, had chosen to continue riding up on the box.

Most of the time Calamity was silent now, apart from her litany of comments regarding the obscure ancestry of each of the horses, and at times she appeared withdrawn; she obviously had something on her mind. Then suddenly she burst out in an accusing tone: 'You're in love with him, aren't you now?'

Startled, Abbie replied, 'I? With whom, may I ask?'

'With Wild Bill!' stated Calamity, almost spitting the words through gritted teeth.

'Most certainly not!' replied Abbie, 'What on earth made you consider such an idea?'

'Well, you were certainly doing a darned lot of whispering together over yonder in the corner of that station back there, an' you weren't discussing the menu!'

Abbie laughed: 'So that's what's been bothering you! You thought I'd developed a crush on Bill Hickok, and I presume that secretly you yourself are sweet on him? Well, you may rest assured that such emotion is the furthest thing from my mind.'

Abashed, Calamity apologized – and then curious, burst out: 'Well, Abbie, but you do have a man though, don't you?'

Abbie shook her head and remained silent, reliving the past. Yes, there had been a man in her life: Tom Wharton, tall and handsome in a rugged masculine way, with his broad sweeping moustache and elegant southern charm, had ridden into her life one fall day, and they had had a whirlwind romance of several months – and then the guns had fired at Fort Sumter. Wharton, a South Carolinian, had felt duty bound to return and offer his services to the Confederacy. He had done so, and had fallen at a place called Gettysburg in Pennsylvania – and romance went out of Abbie's life.

Calamity noticed the reaction her question had caused, and mortified, grabbed Abbie's arm with her left hand. 'Don't you get upset over my joshing you, dearie. There's plenty more fish in the sea, so they tell me. Ha! Git along, yu mobile boneyards!' and the stagecoach hurtled on, at length to arrive in the main and only street of Julesburg, Colorado.

CHAPTER 7

The town had originated as a relay on the Overland Trail to California and was notorious for two incidents. The first was the feud between Jules Beni and Jack Slade, which became a shooting issue. Beni put five bullets into Slade, who survived and vowed revenge. He caught up with Beni, tied him to a fencepost, and mutilated him before killing the man.

The second incident had occurred in 1865 when large bodies of Cheyenne, Arapaho and Lakota Indians had defeated soldiers and civilians defending the town, and returned a week later and burnt every building. By the time of Abbie's arrival, rebuilding had removed most of the scars of the raid.

Leaving their limited luggage with the superintendent of the relay station, the two women sought the livery stable, where Abbie negotiated the purchase of two riding mares, saddles and a sturdy mule as a pack animal. Next, enquiries were made to find if a party was being made up with the intent of going south to the boom town of Denver.

A group of hopeful prospectors was found, preparing to head south to where it was said that gold could be shovelled up by the bucketful. Abbie and Minny, fully independent and carrying their own food, made an arrangement to travel with the gold seekers, merely for the sake of mutual protection.

The party consisted of eight men, only one of whom was a westerner by his accent and by his own account. The other men, two of whom were married, were a mixed group from the British Isles and Europe and included three children under the age of ten. The party had put their limited funds together and had purchased an old wagon and a team of visibly aged oxen. Abbie viewed with concern the breezy air of innocence with which their fellow travellers prepared to hit the trail.

She and Minny had gone to the large tented building being used as a general store, and using Abbie's letter of credit, had bought a supply of food including beans, flour, desiccated vegetables and a side of bacon, as well as coffee, but also two army Enfield rifles (surplus after the recent Civil War), a bag of .577 calibre lead shot, and 5lb of black powder.

There was general agreement to head out at seven o'clock the next morning, and at that time Abbie and Minnie sat astride their horses at the appointed location, with luggage and food, together with coffee pot and frying pan, neatly stowed on the pack animal. And there they sat, with their rifles slung across their shoulders, impatiently waiting whilst the greenhorn party ran around packing and unpacking their goods and chattels, getting in each other's way and all the while creating a general hullabaloo.

Watching the remainder of their party preparing to move out, Abbie and Minny had ample time to observe them and detect their strengths and weaknesses. There were two married men: John Bruce, a Scot with a shrewish wife named Mildred, the possessor of a ready tongue for all who crossed her path; and an Irishman, Pat O'Flynn, with his wife Mary, and their three children Sean, Seamus and Shelagh. There was already bad blood between the two families. The Bruce couple were God-fearing Calvinists, while the O'Flynns were obviously Papists, since Mary the wife was constantly calling upon the saints to preserve them.

Of the five single men, Phil Roberts was English, from London; Hamish MacGregor hailed from the Isle of Bute, and being a Scot, tended to side with his fellow countryman in any dispute; while Kurt Villiers was from Holland, Carl Schmit from Hamburg, and Rudi Jungerson appeared to be Nordic, although he was reticent about his country of origin.

Finally by nine o'clock they were ready to roll, and moved out on to the south track heading towards Denver. The rutted track headed southwest between, on either side, high hills covered in the main with a variety of evergreen foliage. All the people walked either alongside or behind their wagon, or led the plodding oxen – that is, all except their self-appointed leader, who claimed to have a wealth of western trail experience; he rode alone ahead of the group, stating that he was scouting the trail.

Abbie and Minny rode behind the slowly moving wagon with a strong sense of misgiving. Their fellows had adopted a carefree air towards the journey as if they were merely out for a stroll, not a march of nigh on one hundred and fifty miles, with the possibility of encountering hostile natives, even more hostile white men, or extremely adverse weather conditions.

So far Abbie had seen no sign of any one who might be in any way connected with the Jones gang, but she took Wild Bill's warning seriously, and kept a stringent look-out. There had been one occasion in Julesburg when a burly ruffian had shouldered her off the sidewalk into the path of an oncoming wagon, but she had adroitly skipped to one side and the fellow had long since disappeared into the crowd by the time she was back on the boards. Abbie had put his behaviour down to bad manners, and had not pursued the issue. But now, both she and Minny had to be on guard for any kind of incident.

Finally, as the sun sank towards the western horizon, there were calls from some of the more weary of the party that they wanted to make camp, and suggestions were made about finding a suitable glade off the trail. Curiously, Jed Barnaby, their so-called leader, gave no instructions or advice, but just seemed to drift along and fall in with the dominant viewpoint.

At length a halt was called, and in the gathering twilight the travellers prepared to set up camp. Then the first major problem arose. The site chosen for the camp, though free of rocks and with shade from overhanging trees, was dry, with no stream where they could water the stock. To add to their problem the water butt lashed to the side of the wagon was half empty due to careless use during the day. And the nearest stream was half a mile back along the trail.

Abbie let them wrangle among themselves for ten minutes, and then forcibly intervened. Pulling her pistol she fired one shot in the air, crying out 'Quiet!' as she did so.

Startled, the party fell silent, mouths open, looking at her in alarm. Abbie sat on her horse and glared down on them. 'You people are all acting just like a bunch of spoiled children. When are you going to start acting like responsible adults and get organized?'

She paused, and one of the men, bristling with annoyance, seized the moment and burst out: 'What's it got to do with you, lady? Who made you the expert with your money and fancy talk?'

Back in Julesburg, other than stating that her name was Penraven, Abbie had not further identified herself. Now Minny, edging her mare forwards, entered the dispute and cried out: 'You stupid man! You all stupid mans! This here is Pinfire Lady! She already kills many mans and take wagon train to Colorado. Without her . . .' Minny was momentarily silent, seeking some way of emphasizing her point '. . . you all up shit creek!'

Abbie was shocked, yet amused by Minny's violent support, and the man who had challenged her right to criticize the party looked suitably abashed at having challenged a known gunfighter; the others, meanwhile, after talking among themselves, asked Abbie to issue some directions to bring order out of chaos. She did so, instructing the two women to build a fire and prepare food, while the three children gathered dry sticks. Two of the men were ordered to erect a lean-to where their women and children could sleep, and a party guarded by Minny were detailed to drive the oxen up the trail to the stream and water them.

All did as she advised, and order fell upon the camp. While they were busy with their appointed tasks Abbie dismounted and walked over to where Jed Barnaby stood examining his horse's rein with studied interest. She paused, looking at the so-called leader – a middle-aged man with a three-day growth of gingery whiskers concealing his unwashed visage. His slack-jawed appearance hardly indicated a resolute character, and his scruffy apparel suggested that he took little pride in his appearance.

'Jed! You were apparently chosen as leader of this group, but as I see the situation, you haven't done much leading! What's the story?'

Jed shuffled his feet, squinted at the reins, and finally admitted he had been chosen by the men after they had all consumed a few beers and he had unfortunately boasted of his pioneer lore. He further admitted that he had been approached by a stranger in Julesburg and told that he would earn twenty dollars if he took the job. He didn't know why he'd been offered the money, but figured the stranger didn't want the party to get lost and thought Jed could lead them to Denver.

Abbie studied the man for a few moments, and finally came to the conclusion that he was telling the truth. But why would an utter stranger offer money to ensure that this, in reality hopeless individual, was in charge of a small party of greenhorns heading to the diggings? The obvious answer was that the stranger would expect from Jed's incompetence that the party would be delayed in getting to the goldfields – but what could be the purpose in doing that?

Despite turning the situation over and over in her mind Abbie was unable to arrive at a logical conclusion. Meanwhile, under firm guidance and a steady routine, the party rapidly began to assume the qualities of a group of seasoned pioneers. They were tested about two days later when a ragged party of Piutes, men, women and children, approached and begged pitifully for food and above all for whiskey. The men initially flourished their guns, assuming that they were about to be attacked.

Abbie took charge. 'No whiskey! We give red brothers some flour and sugar. All we can share with our friends.' And she told the white women to dole out a small measure of both commodities.

When the Piutes heard Abbie speak they started talking volubly among themselves, gesticulating and expressing visible terms of gratitude. As they shuffled off bearing their small gifts Abbie turned to Minny and asked her what had got the Indians so excited?

'They see you Abbie and they say, "That is Sister Lightning. She is powerful medicine!" They talk about Abbie who take wagon train west and show red brothers how she use guns. They remember. Then because of gifts, they give warning!'

Abbie and most of the group gathered around as Minny explained that further down the trail was a place where a number of 'bad men', mostly whites but also with several native Indians and also a black outlaw, had been holding up, robbing and killing small parties of travellers. In the case of these wayfarers they apparently had an additional incentive since they especially wanted to get the Pinfire Lady in revenge for killing one of their number.

Abbie saw now why Jed Barnaby had been encouraged to lead the party. The more disorganized they were, the less inclined they would be to put up a spirited resistance to any attack. She explained this to the group, and admitted that it was probably her presence that would bring the outlaw gang down upon them. She and Minny could leave, but she doubted whether their absence would vouch safe passage for the remainder.

Abbie fell silent and awaited their decision. With surprise she noted that it was Jed who spoke up.

'Well Ma'am, I think I'm talking for all of us when I stress that if it wasn't for you an' Miss Minny here we wouldn't have got this far, and I reckon that if there's trouble ahead we'll face it together.'

Several of the other men murmured agreement, and one said, 'Just tell us what to do, Miss Abbie, and we'll follow your orders!'

Having thanked them for their confidence in her, Abbie next inquired as to the number of firearms possessed by the party and the degree of confidence they had in their use. The answer to the first question was that seven of the men owned Springfield or Enfield military-style rifles, and three had 10-gauge muzzle-loading shotguns. In addition there were several pistols, revolvers of various calibre, and one single-shot Remington naval piece that was more like a young cannon.

With regard to abilities, the men all claimed a degree of confidence in the use of their individual firearms, with service in the Civil War, and one stated that his wife was also a good shot. Abbie was relieved that apparently she was not starting from scratch in the training of her little command, and she pondered a few minutes, developing a strategy. Then she gathered the people around her.

'Very well! We are a small party travelling by day. During that time the armed men will keep close to the wagon and oxen and no person must wander off – and that includes the children. Meanwhile, Minny and I will scout along in the trees on each side of the trail, hopefully to flush out any would-be ambushers. In the evenings we will use the old trick of eating in relays while half are on guard and then, after making up the fire and leaving suitable dummies lying on the ground, we will repair to chosen positions among the rocks where we can fire down on the campsite if attacked.'

The men nodded in agreement to the plan, impressed that Abbie had made a decision so quickly, and for the next twenty-four hours as they continued along the trail, the whole party was on the alert for any sign of hostile movement ahead or among the rocks and trees off to each side. Then in the late afternoon a sole Piute approached and indicated that he wanted to speak to Minny. With many gesticulations, he dramatically informed them that the outlaws were planning to attack that night. He had been ordered by his chief to crawl close enough to discover their plans, and then to speedily get to Abbie and Minny and warn them of the coming raid. Apparently this gesture was in return for the small items of food they had received from the pioneers.

Armed with such a firm warning, plans were made accordingly.

Abbie chose to site the next camp in a location over-looked by high rocks to the left of the trail. A cleft in the weathered surface of the rocky face led up to a level shelf with sufficient foliage to screen anyone from below. After a hasty meal the campfire was built up and a number of shapes created with blankets to give the appearance of recumbent figures asleep around the blaze. Since the tableau was created between the wagon and oxen and the rock face, Abbie had made a killing zone which she hoped would outweigh any advantage the attackers might have with regard to numbers.

With all arranged to her satisfaction below, Abbie had her people climb up to the shelf thirty feet above ground level, and instructed them to spread out with loaded rifles to cover the campsite. As she did so, she reminded each shooter that, since he would be firing down at about 45 degrees, he should aim low at his target. With one last instruction to wait until she gave the word, she and Minny descended; having moved the four riding animals to a safe location back up the trail, the two women squatted down by the wall of rock, fairly confident that they were out of the line of fire.

Time passed slowly as darkness fell, and the campfire blaze died back to glowing embers. Luckily it was a night of a full moon, which cast its glow on the peaceful scene. All was quiet apart from the occasional cry of some noc-turnal creature, either hunter or hunted. Then to the south could be heard the muffled sound of hoofbeats, fol-lowed by a few moments of silence; the riders had obviously dismounted, as there were shuffling sounds and a low muttered curse followed by a 'Shh' as shadowy figures with pistols raised crept towards their sleeping victims.

Reaching the campsite, with a gesture from their leader the would-be killers spread out, and at a further signal all opened fire simultaneously. As the crashing roll of gunfire rolled away, Abbie took aim at the figure of the man who appeared to be the leader and cried out: 'Now, men! Fire!' and squeezed the trigger of her Pinfire revolver as she did so. Her target was hurled backwards into the campfire as the riflemen answering her command fired, the sound echoing back and forth among the hills as the killers died in a hail of lead.

The raiding party had consisted of a dozen men, and in the fierce burst of fire from the eight rifles and Abbie's and Minny's pistols, ten of the attackers fell. Abbie's instruction had been to fire, reload, and finish off any unwounded or potential enemies still capable of causing mayhem. The eleventh attacker turned to run and fell to Abbie's second shot, and of the raiding party one solitary figure stumbled away into the darkness and shortly after could be heard riding furiously down the trail.

As the long night passed, the travellers at Abbie's suggestion remained in their elevated position while she and Minny walked among the still bodies with pistols drawn prepared to finish off any who were still breathing. There was no need. The ambuscade had proven to be very effective, and as a pearly dawn rose in the east, the remainder of the group descended and all the bodies were dragged to lie in a line against the wall of rocks.

At Jed's suggestion the gruesome task was undertaken to search the corpses for any identification, or anything to indicate from where they originated. Soon a small pile of pitiful objects was accumulated: two decks of greasy playing cards, four or five clasp knives, loose change in various currencies, a broken rosary, tobacco and several pipes. There was nothing to indicate the names of the men, and only one piece of paper among them, which appeared to have been part of a letter written in some unknown language.

Since after the night's work none were desirous of staying for breakfast in the glade of death, preparations were being made to pack the shot-torn blankets in the wagon and continue the journey, when a fresh group of riders rode in from the south led by a grim-faced man wearing a star.

'Hold it right there, folks! Nobody's doing any moving 'til we find out what's been going on here!'

Then he noticed the line of bodies, and a pistol magically appeared in his hand: 'Maybe I'll amend that last statement! Now I'd like you all to lay down your weapons and back up against that there wagon!'

A feminine voice interrupted the remainder of his orders. 'Does that include me, Marshal Thompson?' and he swung his horse around to see Abbie Penraven smiling at him.

'The Pinfire Lady, by all the powers! I haven't seen you since we went down to Texas together. What on earth are you doing here? Last I heard you was over in England?' And Abbie, after telling her people that everything was all right, gave a detailed account to Marshal Thompson and his Denver posse of all that had happened since they had left Julesburg.

When Abbie had completed her account, the marshal removed his sombrero and scratched his head. 'Well! If that doesn't beat anything! This foreigner rode into Denver in the middle of the night screeching that his friends, innocent travellers, were being brutally attacked, and pleaded for help, so this posse was formed and here we are – only the facts are the other way around.'

'And what happened to your informant?' Queried Abbie.

'Well, he said he was going to rally more men and would join us here to help capture all these desperadoes.'

'Though of course, as we all know, by now he, on a fresh horse, probably donated by the good people of Denver, is no doubt many miles from the scene of the action.'

Ruefully, Marshal Thompson smiled down at Abbie and admitted that she was, as usual, probably right.

With that remark he motioned to the posse and they headed south to Denver, with the final remark that he would send men to bury the corpses of the bandits, and meanwhile the group could proceed with their journey.

The rest of the journey to Denver, or rather to Cherry Creek, was uneventful, and as they reached the rapidly expanding urban area, Abbie and Minny bade farewell to their travelling companions, who were loud in their gratitude for the way in which Abbie had handled their problems.

CHAPTER 8

Abbie made enquiries regarding accommodation, and from the limited choice available, they decided on The Kansas House run by a Mrs Dolman, a grey-haired, plump little lady of Germanic origin, who liked to claim that her inn was the first one in Denver. It was primitive in the extreme, but the landlady claimed that she could provide a private room with access to a bath, and her bread, pies and cookies, sold to the miners, suggested that the cooking was palatable.

Having bathed, Abbie and Minny donned their old range clothing as it had been decided to do some exploring in the Denver neighbourhood. Abbie was curious about the sheet of paper found on one of the bandits who had attacked the party with whom she had travelled to Denver, and once again examined it closely. On one side of the folded sheet was a pencilled sketchmap which she thought could be interpreted without too much difficulty.

The map showed a line labelled Cherry Creek and another similarly marked North Platte, with an arrow indicating a large N for north. A dotted line going south-west from a square marked D to an illustration, obviously indicating a building, apparently showed a route for someone, but who? What was equally mysterious was the fact that the dotted line was marked 22V.

The other side of the paper was apparently the last page of a letter, but was in no language that Abbie had encountered, and curiously the message, if such was its purpose, was signed in a totally different manner than the script above. She had to locate somebody who might be able to translate the contents of the sheet or at least give her some idea of its significance.

She spoke to their landlady. 'Mrs Dolman, you encounter many people who buy your wares, or who have resided at the Kansas House. Do you recall anyone who might understand foreign languages?'

Mrs Dolman shook her head dubiously, not too sure what Abbie was seeking. Then her face brightened. 'There is one such man. All the other miners call him the professor. He has a claim down on the creek, but he don't often work it 'cos he's drunk most of the time.'

Abbie obtained directions on how to find the man she sought, and she and Minny, retrieving the horses from the livery stable, rode out to try and find the elusive professor. A ride of a couple of miles brought them to a little stream that emptied into Cherry Creek, and there on the bank was a ramshackle 'soddy' with flowers growing on the earthen roof. There was but one window, which was merely a piece of grimy glass set in a hole in the wall on the left of the door, which was sagging drunkenly on leather hinges.

Abbie dismounted and tapped on the door. There was

no sound within. She knocked louder, using the butt of her pistol. This time there was a response, as a drunken voice snarled that whoever was making that infernal racket should desist and go to a much warmer place.

Compressing her lips, Abbie raised her Pinfire and put a shot into the roofing above the door. This produced a positive reaction, as the door was flung open, revealing a scantily dressed male figure who stood there and roared at them in an upper class English accent, 'Blast you to blazes! Can't a body obtain a limited degree of tranquillity without strangers hooting, hollering, and discharging volleys of firearms in his general vicinity?'

Then, realizing that he was addressing a woman, accompanied by yet another female, he paused with surprise; cutting a rather ridiculous figure in a long pair of dirty ragged underpants, topped with an equally filthy vest, he made a handsome bow and apologized for his attire, indicating that his manservant was absent with the laundry. Staggering to a little bench beside the doorway he put his hands on his head, groaned, and said, 'Now ladies, what can I do for you? If it's money that you are seeking I'm afraid my remittance is sadly overdue this quarter. On the other hand, if you are desiring to save my soul I'm afraid you're about thirty years too late.'

Abbie assured him that they were seeking neither his money nor his soul, but merely wished to obtain some information – and produced the mysterious sheet of notepaper.

He glanced at the sketchmap, and turning the paper over, looked at the script and chuckled, 'Why it's child's play! This chappie has written his letter in classical Greek, and even then I can spot at least three errors. The signature is that of one Nikolai Stroganoff written in Cyrillic lettering. Incidentally, the sketch map shows 22V on it. I would suggest that distance is Russian. Twenty-two verst. A verst is about two thirds of a mile. Therefore about fifteen or possibly sixteen miles.

'As to the letter itself, well, we only have the last page, but apparently this Russian chap is warning his friends Hiram P. Markover and Sir Bertram Wallace that their project is endangered and that he was going to take care of one Lady Abigail Penraven, otherwise known as the Pinfire Lady. Would you happen to be the lady in question, my dear?'

Abbie nodded, took the notepaper, and thanked the professor with a warning not to mention this matter to anyone; she and Minny then rode back to The Kansas House. Abbie was still pondering on the information contained in the portion of the letter in her pocket when she found a gentleman waiting to see her.

Directly she saw him Abbie recognized the visitor, who announced himself: 'It's Gotwald, Roger Gotwald! Lady Penraven, may I speak to you privately?' this was voiced with a sideways glance at Minny, who stood there expressionless.

'Mr Gotwald, there is no need for my friend Minny to leave. She is privy to all that concerns me. How have you been doing since we all left London?'

Abbie suggested that the three of them should repair to a more private room, but before they could do so Marshal Thompson burst into The Kansas House. 'Abbie Penraven! What have you and this little Ute friend of yours been up to? I've just left the shack of poor old Professor Muggeridge and he's lying there with his throat cut from ear to ear. An' the neighbours all around tell me that you two ladies were asking questions of him just a couple of hours ago! What have you been up to?' and he stood, hands on hips, glaring at the two women.

Abbie looked at Gotwald, and suggested that the marshal should join them in a conference; so they went up to the girls' room, where she described their visit to Muggeridge and what he said was contained in the note. She then looked towards Roger Gotwald to see what he could add to the situation.

Gotwald had travelled from London to Washington where other American agents had shared their information about Stroganoff's contacts, and how it would seem that all activity was moving towards the west coast. It was reported that Hiram Markover had not been seen in his usual haunts in New York, and that the other member of the unholy trio, Sir Bertram Wallace, was said to be directing operations to eliminate a certain female who had interfered with his plans.

Abbie cast her mind back. During the episode of Minny's rescue from the Black Cat she had noticed that one of the men in the upper room with Sykes had spoken with a guttural foreign accent, but she had thought little of it at the time as London abounded with foreigners. He had probably survived the encounter and duly reported to Wallace, and probably also to Hiram Markover – hence the vendetta against her.

Upon mentioning this reasoning to Gotwald, he nodded in agreement. 'You are undoubtedly right, Abbie.

Hiram Markover is known to be associated with criminal elements in the United States, and probably Canada too, for that matter. The attack by the Reno gang upon the train on which you were travelling may have had a two-fold purpose: robbery and deliberate murder. Likewise the attempted hold-up of the stagecoach by elements of the Jones gang: robbery and the elimination of someone they were assured was an enemy. The more recent attack on the trail from Julesburg was even more horrendous, since these criminals were prepared to murder a whole group of people to attain their goal.'

Abbie interjected, 'But what is the significance of Denver? I can understand their animosity towards me as a possible adversary, but their sketchmap, if that's what it is, seems to suggest that some activity is to take place in this area!'

'Well, I don't know what you folks are going to do, but I've got a cruel murder to solve, so I'm going to make more enquiries along Cherry Creek – and also, if you don't object, I'll send one of my best deputies to check out the area about twenty miles to the southwest. Burt Stevens is a good man – I know he'll be careful.' With that last remark Marshal Thompson departed, leaving Abbie and Gotwald uncertain as to their next course of action.

CHAPTER 9

They didn't have too long to wait. As they were discussing the whereabouts of the sinister trio, namely Stroganoff, Markover and Wallace, and whether it was possible that they were actually in the Denver area, a man came into The Kansas House seeking Abbie, 'S'cuse me, lady! There's a man in Mattie Silk's place saying that he's going to shoot all the girls and burn the place down if you don't come down there and surrender to him.'

'Thanks for delivering your message, my good man. Now, who is Mattie Silk and where is her place located? Furthermore, who is the man from whom you got the message?'

'Well, Mattie's just recently arrived in Denver and has opened a house for young ladies,' he smirked at Roger Gotwald '. . . if you know what I mean!' winking furiously. 'It's down on Larimer Street. You can't miss it. She has a red lantern hanging outside!'

The man turned to leave and Abbie called him back, 'One moment! Who gave you the message?'

'Amos Jones, from Missouri! He's a deadly killer and

says he's seeking revenge, cos you killed his brother!' And with that he scurried from the inn.

Roger Gotwald spoke up. 'Of course you're going to ignore this ridiculous summons, Abbie?'

Abbie shook her head slowly. 'No, Roger I can't! To do so would mean he is still on my trail and also, if I refuse to fight, the word will soon get around and every would-be gunfighter will come looking for me, to make a name for himself. No! Sadly, I must face him! But we'll see if I can find an edge, as Billy Curtis would have said. Minny and I have to do some scouting.'

The two women left, and rode slowly to the unpaved Larimer Street. After noticing the red lantern, but not stopping, they turned left, and then left again on to McGaa Street, until they located the back of Mattie Silk's boarding house for young ladies. Her establishment fortunately backed on to a livery stable, and as dusk fell, Abbie and Minny stabled their horses there and approached the rear of Mattie's 'business'.

It was a two-storey building roughly thrown together in frontier fashion. There were no windows on the ground floor, just a closed door, but on the upper floor were several small windows lit with candlelight.

Abbie tried the door, which evidently opened outwards; it moved slightly, and she noticed that it hung on two leather hinges, the same as Muggeridge's 'soddy'.

The girls drew their Bowie knives and made short work of slicing through the leather. Then, carefully, they lifted the door down and leaned it against the wall. Entering, they found themselves in a scullery, with a narrow stairway leading to the second floor. Creeping up it they came to a long landing with doors on both sides. All was silent, but as they crept along, one door opened, and a girl, dressed in nothing but a filmy negligée, slipped out – but when she encountered the two pistol-bearing females, she stopped with one hand over her mouth.

Abbie motioned her back into the room. All three entered and Minny shut the door quietly.

'What is your name, girl?' whispered Abbie in her most authoritative voice, 'and where are the rest of the inhabitants?' As she asked these questions, Abbie looked about her with sad interest. The girl was called Belle, and her room was small, with just enough space for a little mirror-backed dressing table, strewn with toiletries and trinkets, a single chair, an open closet in which hung some outdoor clothing, and a bed where Belle no doubt earned her living.

In whispered tones Belle answered Abbie's questions. Earlier in the evening they had all been called down to the parlour, where they usually met 'gentlemen friends', to find Madam Silk, for so she described herself, being covered with a big gun by a bearded man, while another kept the front door closed and motioned would-be clients away. Belle, terrified, had thrown up, and after some argument had been permitted to go up to her room.

From Belle, Abbie gained a general idea of the layout of the parlour and its inhabitants. A wide stairway led down to the back wall of the room, the left side of which contained a bar. There were two couches where the other five girls were sitting, scared out of their wits, and several plush armchairs, one of which was to the right of the main door. That one was occupied by Mattie Silk. When Belle was permitted to go upstairs, the man with the gun was standing to Mattie's left with his pistol resting on her shoulder.

Abbie whispered instructions to Minny, and told Belle to remain in her room; the scared girl gladly complied. Then the pair slipped silently to the stair-head, Abbie with holstered pistol, while Minny, who, though accurate, was slow on the draw, had her .36 Navy Colt firmly gripped in her right hand. Then, taking a deep breath, Abbie, followed closely by Minny, stepped slowly down the stairs. As she came into view to the people below, she addressed the gunman:

'Good evening Amos. I don't think that I've had the dubious pleasure of meeting you before. I hear that you think you can outdraw me in a fair fight. Is that so?'

Abbie had gambled on his gunman's pride that he could and would outdraw her, and he proceeded to holster his pistol, a large .44 calibre Remington. (If he had raised the gun towards the stairway Minny was to shoot. If not, she would cover the character by the door.)

Amos Jones grinned wolfishly, revealing yellow, broken teeth, and wiped the back of his hand across his tobacco-stained moustache.

'So you're the Pinfire Lady who's had such a reputation in the west! Well, Missee, I figure on cutting you down to size, so let's get to it!' and as he said these final words his hand flashed to his right hip where nestled his big Remington. His gun was half raised when Abbie's revolver bellowed and spoke again twice more. Three crimson blotches appeared in Jones's chest: his pistol hung momentarily by the trigger guard before dropping to the carpeted floor, followed moments later by its owner.

Abbie's shots had been followed by those of Minny, who

neatly disposed of the guard by the door. There was complete silence as the grey acrid smoke curling from their guns drifted towards the ceiling, and then excited chatter broke out from the assembled girls, and Mattie Silk breathed a long, visible sigh of relief. (After this episode Mattie took to packing a pistol herself, and later it was reported that she had a duel with a rival madam, actually shooting her opponent in what the newspapers referred to as 'the public [sic] arch'.)

Despite the pool of blood staining her brand new carpet Mattie Silk was profuse in her gratitude to both Abbie and Minny, saying to the former: 'Honey! If you ever want a change of occupation you're always welcome here at any time!' To which offer Abbie, stifling a smile, gravely declined. Then she and Minny left to collect their horses and return to The Kansas House.

Their arrival relieved the anxiety of Roger Gotwald, who apparently had spent the whole time of their absence restlessly pacing up and down; the trio gathered in the girls' room to decide on their next course of action. On the positive side, the Jones gang, as a part of an international conspiracy, appeared to be finished, and that, together with the defeat of both the coach robbers and the mob which had attacked the travellers, had to be considered successes. But the murder of Professor Muggeridge, and thereby the elimination of a source of possible information, had to be considered as a loss.

Both Abbie and Gotwald felt as though they were floundering: they knew they were on the brink of a potential international crisis involving the United States, Russia, and probably Great Britain, yet they were incapable of doing anything about the situation. Where was the unsavoury international trio, and what was the significance of Denver?

Abbie suggested that they repair to the dining room and partake of a meal prepared by Mrs Dolman as a way of taking their minds off what she described as the 'Denver conundrum'. This they did, and while waiting for the ordered meal to arrive, Abbie picked up the latest edition of *The Rocky Mountain News*, idly glancing at the advertisements for mining equipment, livestock, guns and land being offered and sold. Suddenly her attention was riveted by a column stating that the Eldorado mine was shipping two million dollars in gold.

That was it! Quickly she drew Gotwald's attention to the news item: 'Roger, what does every international venture require above all other elements? Money!' she answered her own question. 'With money one can buy ships, arms, men, influence and, if required, adequate bribes where people will look the other way when it is necessary that they do so!'

CHAPTER 10

The following morning Abbie, Minny and Roger Gotwald rode out to the Eldorado mine, located three miles into the hills to the west of Denver. After being stopped by a dozen rifle-bearing mine guards, they finally got to see the owner, Abe Rawlings, and his mine superintendent, a surly Cornishman named Bill Pengelly. Abbie allowed Gotwald to do the introductions, since he was representing the President of the United States. Abbie was introduced merely as the Pinfire Lady and Minny as her friend.

Without any reference to any international conspiracy, Roger stated that having seen in the paper that a large quantity of gold was being shipped shortly, and since government sources had been advised that an attempt might well be made to seize the shipment, it was thought proper to liaise with the mine owner and ensure that the shipment was well guarded.

Abe Rawlings, a white-haired man who seemed overwhelmed by his sudden good fortune, expressed his appreciation of the Federal interest in the security of his gold shipments, but then turned to Pengelly: 'What do you think, Bill? After all, you, not I, are in charge of all security arrangements?'

Pengelly was far more negative. 'Abe! We swore that we wouldn't discuss the gold shipments with anybody. Now I reckon we can trust this fella who works for the Federal government. But I don't think that we should say anything in front of these two women. Women talk! They can't help it. It's just part of their nature. Now this one,' indicating Abbie, 'is supposed to be some kind of gunfighter, if you believe the stories, but that doesn't give her any kind of credential in my eyes.'

Abbie pursed her lips and prepared to make a tart response to Pengelly's comments, but since they had previously agreed that Roger Gotwald would do the talking she bit her tongue and remained silent.

Pengelly brought the interview to an abrupt end when he said dismissively: 'If any kind of trouble arises we will certainly call for help. Until that time, thank you for the visit. Good day to you!'

With that remark Pengelly turned and walked away to his office, followed by a bemused employer more than slightly startled by the man's behaviour.

The trio rode slowly back to Denver. For a while there was silence – an embarrassed silence on the part of Roger Gotwald, who belatedly thought that he should have spoke up in defence of Abbie. She meanwhile was boiling internally with anger that Pengelly had chosen to characterize her and Minny in such a negative manner. Minny, knowing instinctively that Abbie was annoyed with the rude white man, fingered her Bowie knife in a manner that boded ill for Bill Pengelly should she meet him in a dark alley.

Eventually, Abbie broke the silence with the remark that she felt Pengelly's attitude was strange when compared with that of his employer. Was that his natural demeanour, or was there something more? Roger agreed with Abbie's assessment. Both came to the same conclusion: namely that Rawlings the mine owner somehow appeared very subdued, even cowed compared with his obnoxious employee.

Then Minny supplied the information which could be the key to the mine situation. With her keen eyesight she had spotted a man concealed in the slag heap observing the meeting – and that man had a rifle aimed at Abe Rawlings!

The conclusion reached was that Pengelly, and presumably also the mine guards, had taken control of the mine, and that Abe Rawlings was a hostage brought out as cover for their activities. How this criminal activity, if indeed it was such, fitted into what they were beginning to think of as the 'Alaska Connection' remained to be seen.

They rode to Marshal Thompson's office seeking information, and were fortunately able to find him available, though preoccupied with problems of his own.

Abbie opened their inquiry with the question: 'Marshal, what can you tell us about Abe Rawlings and the Eldorado mine operation?' The marshal replied:

'Well, Abbie! Rawlings appeared in the Denver area about eighteen months ago and staked a claim off Cherry Creek. It didn't produce much in the way of pay dirt, but he seemed happy enough. Then he staked another claim out where the Eldorado is, and this time he struck it rich. And as so often happens, it changed him. Whereas before he would come into town, chat with folks in the stores, have a drink or so and generally act sociable, now he acted more like a recluse, leaving everything to his mine superintendent, that Bill Pengelly. Least that was the impression I got when I dropped by the mine when making a circuit up that way.'

Roger Gotwald posed the question as to whether Rawlings could be acting under some kind of a threat from Pengelly, suggesting that just maybe there was something in Rawlings' past which was now being held over him and causing him to act in a manner contrary to his previous behaviour.

While these discussions were taking place, two deputy marshals rode up to the office, leading a third horse with a body draped across the saddle. Marshal Thompson glanced out of the window of his office, visibly startled, and dashed out, followed by his guests. 'That's Burt Stevens' bronc! What happened?' He demanded, looking up at the two grim-faced riders.

'Well, Frank, since we hadn't heard any word from Burt we decided to follow his trail to the south-west to see if there was any sign of him. About fifteen miles out we spied this body hanging from a pine tree. Riding closer we discovered it was poor Burt Stevens. He had been tortured and then hung, with this note pinned to his shirt: "Death to all spies!" We checked around but could see nothing else so we cut Burt down and returned. Sorry Boss! Burt was a good man!'

'OK Joe! Take Burt's body along to the undertaker's, and then you and Marty go get some shut-eye, you deserve it.'

Frank Thompson then stated that he was riding out to the site of the hanging to see if there were any clues that might have been missed, and Abbie and company gladly volunteered to accompany him.

Thompson brought along five other deputies, and the nine riders made a sombre journey out to where a piece of rope still dangled from a stout branch of a towering pine. The party rode and walked the area looking for anything which would assist them in identifying the murderer. On the scuffled pine-needle strewn surface there wasn't even a hand-rolled cigarette butt.

Minny was the person who furnished a lead. She had ridden in ever widening circles in an effort to pick up the trail, and finally returned to where the group of riders was sitting glumly facing the fact that they had failed. She had a small smile on her face as she whispered something to Abbie.

'Hold on men! I think Minny may have something important to say. Go ahead Minny!'

Minny grinned, and said loudly; 'No sheep!' All the men stared at her with puzzled looks. She pointed towards the adjoining hillside and its cover of grass. 'Field has plenty sheep turds, but no sheep! Me think sheep-man see something bad. He take sheep and go damn fast!'

Frank Thompson grasped what Minny was driving at. 'So you're saying that the shepherd may have actually seen the hanging? Well, there's only one way to find out, and that's to follow that flock.'

So saying, Frank urged his horse to a trot, and with a light touch of the spur took up the trail of the missing woollies, followed by the rest of the party – except for

Minny herself, who moved rapidly out in front, appointing herself trail leader, causing Abbie to smile, since it was unusual for the Ute girl to take the lead in any endeavour.

The direction taken by the flock was not hard to follow because of the short-cropped grass and the number of sheep droppings. In less than an hour's ride they heard the baa-baaing of many sheep, and topping the next rise beheld the flock spread out across the next hillside.

Then a curious thing happened. A male figure dressed in a multi-coloured poncho, off-white pants and wearing a straw sombrero looked up, saw the oncoming riders, and fled, presumably in terror, towards the shelter of a rocky outcrop.

Abbie and Minny gave chase, with the former yelling at the top of her voice; 'Stop! Hold on there! We mean you no harm, *amigo*!'

Whether it was the female voice, the term of amigo (friend), or the basic fact that he just couldn't outrun the horses and reach the shelter of the rocks before them, the shepherd stopped running and waited apprehensively as they rode up.

Abbie strove to put the man at his ease. '*Buenos dias, señor*! What is your name?'

He remained silent, so Abbie volunteered some information about herself; '*Me llamo* Abbie Penraven. *Soy inglesa.*' Having offered the fact that she was British and given her name, Abbie lapsed back into English, as her knowledge of Spanish was exhausted.

Finally she received a reply: '*Señorita*! I am called Juan Garcia. I look after sheep of Señor McVie.'

'And where is Señor McVie, Señor Garcia?'

Garcia shrugged his shoulders. 'I do not know, *señorita.* Some days ago he went away and he is not come back yet.'

'Then why did you try to run away when you saw us coming, Juan?'

'Señorita Abbie! I am just a poor Mexicano. I do not understand many things that happen here lately.'

Juan explained in his broken English how two days ago a man had ridden by with just a smile and a greeting. Later the same day this man had been brought back by two others. Bad things had been done to him and upon reaching the big pine tree they had put a rope around his neck and hanged him. Then leaving his horse grazing, they had ridden away laughing.

The sheep were further up the hillside when the bad deed was done, and he himself had been having a little sleep under the bushes quite close to the tree, but he did not think that the men had seen him. 'Many Americanos they see us, but do not see us,' he explained, meaning that Mexican *peons* were just part of the landscape. Later, however, he had thought more, and was frightened that they would come back and kill him, so he was moving the flock and himself to safety when the *señorita* and her friend rode up.

Upon being asked if he could describe the men, Juan did so, and when asked if he would go with the posse and if he saw the murderers point them out, he remained silent – then looking at Abbie and receiving a little nod of her head, he sighed and said he would go. One of the deputies, to his obvious disgust, was told to hand over his horse to Juan, and thus mounted, the whole posse rode south-west on the trail of Burt Steven's killers.

As they rode, the terrain grew ever more mountainous with lofty crags and soaring cliffs, and the trail led upwards through a narrow canyon, which several members observed would be a perfect place for an ambush.

Rounding a rocky curve the party was brought up short by a breast-high stone wall stretching the full width of the canyon; the trail led to a stout gate, now closed, in its centre. Several rifle-armed men were present, and as the riders approached they took defensive positions behind the wall.

For a moment it looked as though there was a stand-off, and Marshal Thompson quickly told his posse that he would do the talking.

'Hello there! Marshal Frank Thompson speaking! Who's the head man here?'

At his query a lean, bearded man dressed in a dark shirt and pants and wearing a Stetson bearing some device sauntered forwards; spitting a stream of tobacco juice on the ground, he said that he was the head honcho, and intimated that their boss didn't take too kindly to strangers unless they had an invitation. He countered this with the remark:

'No offence, Marshal! It's just one of Mr Stroganoff's little ways. My name is Jim Fagin. What can we do for you? The boss is always eager to assist the law.'

Frank had rapidly summed up the situation, and realized that since they were covered by close on a dozen rifles, the wrong reply could result in the immediate slaughter of his whole posse; he therefore had to create a fictitious scenario.

'Well, Jim, we're hunting a bunch of no-good bandits

who held up and robbed the Denver bank yesterday, killing the teller and four customers in the process. They headed south-west from town, and this fella' – indicating Juan – 'saw the four of them go past his place. He thought they looked like fellow greasers, so I brought him along to identify them. However, seeing that this is obviously a box canyon, they couldn't have come this way, so we'll have to back-track and see if we can pick up their trail.'

And with a final 'S'long Jim,' Marshal Thompson turned his horse and, accompanied by the rest of the posse, rode slowly back around the shoulder of the rocky cliff and headed back down the trail, not drawing rein until he was a full mile away from the barricaded area. Then he halted and gathered the group around.

'Time for a little pow-wow men, not to mention you two ladies,' he said, bowing gracefully to Abbie and Minny. 'What did we see and hear back there?'

Roger Gotwald was the first to respond: 'Well, I reckon that we know where Nikolai Stroganoff resides when he's in the country, if that fort back there is his domain.'

'Did anybody notice the badge on Jim Fagin's stetson? To me it looked like a bird with two heads holding a bolt of lightning in its claws. I'm sure that has a Russian significance,' offered Abbie.

Even Juan spoke up hesitantly: 'The men wore the same clothes as the ones who killed Meester Stevens, I think.'

Frank Thompson nodded his head in agreement: 'You are right, Juan. And it's curious that the guards at the Eldorado mine wear the same type of clothing and have that same device pinned on their headgear.'

Minny had meanwhile been whispering to Abbie, and

the latter stated, 'Well, Minny, that could be of importance. Speak up!'

And Minny, gaining the attention of the posse, said:
'Did any mans see little path maybe made by mountain
goat or sheeps high up on cliff?' she indicated the left
side, 'I think maybe mans could get along path in dark
time if making an attack.'

The posse members were profuse in their praise of
Minny for seeing something they had missed. They had all
been concentrating on the men, while Minny had ignored
the men and considered a method of a possible attack.

Abbie advised that, since the occupants of what she
called Fort Stroganoff would no doubt be on their guard
due to the posse's recent visit, perhaps they should instead
make another call at the mine and attempt to clarify the
situation there. There was a general agreement to Abbie's
suggestion, and the whole party, including Juan Garcia,
headed towards the Eldorado mine.

CHAPTER 11

Before the objective was in sight Marshal Thompson divided the posse into two groups. He, Gotwald, Abbie and Minny, having been to the site before and being familiar with the location, were to be the advance party. Meanwhile, the remainder of the deputies and Juan were to make a wide sweep and approach the area from the rear once they heard gunshots.

The four riders of the advance party rode up openly and, as expected, Bill Pengelly came out to meet them. Rawlings, however, the mine owner, was not in sight.

'Now what's the problem, Marshal? I can't spend all day chatting to visitors, y'know!'

Frank Thompson prepared to descend from his horse only to be halted by Pengelly. 'I'm sorry Frank, but you'll have to come back. I'm far too busy with problems of my own to waste time when I should be working!'

As he said this last remark Abbie had edged her horse forward and slipped from the saddle behind Pengelly. Thus with the mine superintendent in front of her and her horse immediately behind she was partially concealed from the watching mine guards as she drew her pistol and stuck it none too gently against Pengelly's spine.

'Mr Pengelly! I believe they call this a Mexican stand-off. If you make an adverse move you get a 12mm bullet in your backbone!' As she said this she twisted the muzzle of her Pinfire revolver in his loose clothing. The increased pressure causing him to wince and suck in his breath with an involuntary 'sss'! 'Now, I want you to call all of your guards out here, and when they are gathered we will have them lay down their arms. Tell them to ignore a single pistol shot. And you'd better sound convincing or you're a dead man!'

As she spoke she slid the muzzle of her pistol up and down Pengelly's spine, and in an unsteady voice he complied with her instructions.

The mine guards came forth reluctantly from their various hiding places, obedient to the orders of a superior in their organization, and when all had been accomplished, Frank Thompson fired a single shot. Minutes later the deputies arrived; they dismounted, and then their guns also had the mine guards covered. Then and only then was a disarmed Bill Pengelly permitted to join his men, now lined up on identification parade. Juan Garcia looked at the prisoners intently: 'That man, Señor Marshal!' pointing to the third man from the left. 'He was one of the men who killed Señor Stevens!'

The guard identified, a swarthy fellow with a cast in the left eye, started at being so easily identified, and with a muttered curse of, 'I'll get you, you stinkin' greaser!' his right hand swooped downwards to grab his Remington percussion revolver.

But Abbie's hand was faster to draw her Pinfire pistol just recently holstered. Even as his right hand closed upon the grip of his gun, Abbie's pistol spoke twice, and he was hurled backwards as two soft lead bullets smashed into his chest. The other guards' hands shot skywards, and they stood, startled, at the sight of the slightly built woman before them gently waving her heavy calibre handgun back and forth before them as though inviting anyone to try and succeed where their compatriot had failed.

Their hands tied behind them with pigging string, the other guards and Pengelly were herded away, and Abbie and Gotwald went in search of Abe Rawlings. They found him locked in a small windowless storeroom, hungry, thirsty and dishevelled, with several days' growth of beard obscuring his features.

He told them a sorry tale of how Pengelly had wheedled himself into his confidence and also that of his wife, now held prisoner at Fort Stroganoff as insurance for his good behaviour. Because Abe had recently exhibited signs of rebellion he had been locked up in the room in which he was found.

Interrogating the prisoners one by one, they pieced together a great deal about the routine at Fort Stroganoff – from one, the number of guards; from another the routine; and from several, that Stroganoff, Hiram Markover and Sir Bertram Wallace were currently in residence.

The Eldorado mine was not the bonanza it had been heralded to be. True, it was modestly successful, but in actual fact most of the gold in the strongroom came from raids and robberies carried out right across Colorado. The intent was to move all the gold in bulk with a large escort to a port on the west coast. Thereafter its destination was unknown.

Abbie suggested that they hold an impromptu council of war to assess the situation, to which the others agreed.

'Well, Roger, first of all the information you have received that certain parties are attempting to thwart Mr Seward's plan to purchase Alaska for the United States would certainly seem to have been corroborated by what we have learned and also experienced. Stroganoff is at the centre of a plot, international in nature, which therefore also involves the United Kingdom, since, with the connivance of Wallace, they intend to seize British territory. This in turn involves me, since as you well know I would appear to be a person representing British interests in this area. Then we have Frank Thompson, the representative of local law and order, and there is yourself representing the Federal government. Now, to take Fort Stroganoff, would we need some kind of legal warrant, and also military aid, if such were available?'

'I can answer part of that, Abbie,' Frank Thompson stated. 'As a marshal, investigating the murder of one of my deputies, I have the right to search premises and question suspects anywhere around Denver. The problem is that we now know the fort has a garrison of possibly as many as sixty men, and I can't rustle up more then ten or twelve men to act as deputies. We therefore definitely need military support . . .' and he looked towards Roger Gotwald as the senior Federal representative for an answer.

'Well, I agree with you, Frank,' answered Roger, 'But I

don't know where we can get any aid around here at short notice.'

One of the deputies spoke up: 'There's a military hunting party about ten miles from here. After bighorns I reckon. Maybe they'd lend a hand if we ask them.'

Abbie intervened: 'Look, gentlemen. I know that additional aid is required and may make all the difference if we make a frontal assault. But perhaps we should reconnoitre and see if there is any feature that would assist us. This is what I propose.

'Firstly, Minny and I noticed that the narrow ledge on the left-hand cliff face extends around the bulge in the rock, therefore anyone who can ascend to that position cannot be seen from below. We are suggesting that come nightfall, Minny will somehow get up to that ledge and determine how far it extends beyond their wall.

'Secondly, we might augment the influence of our limited numbers if we can obtain some explosives. I know that during our Crimean War British soldiers made grenades from soda bottles filled with gunpowder, and I believe that in the late civil war both sides made similar improvised munitions. I imagine that being a mine, gunpowder should be readily available, and also bottles and cans in which to put our explosive materials. So I suggest we scavenge around and see what we can devise.

'Meanwhile, by all means send someone to see if the hunting party can assist us. Roger, perhaps you'd better undertake that task as the Federal representative.'

The assembled men, after their initial surprise at the confident way this female rapidly summed up their situation, and the sensible military solutions she proposed, fell to and carried out her directions. Roger Gotwald, accompanied by the deputy who knew where the military party was located, rode off to try and enlist their help. Abe Rawlings directed others to a shed set apart from other buildings where he had stored the gunpowder used in his mining operations; while two more made their way to the area behind the cookhouse, where they found an abundance of garbage, among which were many cans and bottles ideal for their purpose.

Of equal importance was the fact that one of the deputies, a Union army veteran, had been adept at constructing grenades during his military service, and was delighted with the opportunity to exhibit his skills to his fellows.

Meanwhile Abbie and Minny cut up blankets to create crude boots to put over their horses' hoofs in order to muffle their footfall during their night-time approach. It had earlier been decided that Minny would scale the rocks and explore the ledge, while Abbie remained below tending the two horses and keeping guard.

In late afternoon the two girls rode away, with cries of good luck ringing in their ears, to get to within a mile of their objective before night fell. Fortunately there was a long twilight, and they rested in a small grove of aspens, fitting on their horses' hoof wear and waiting for full darkness.

Eventually, under a full moon and a star-spangled sky, they rode slowly and cautiously forwards along the trail that led to Fort Stroganoff, halting when thy reached a cleft perhaps fifty yards short of the bulge of rock which hid the stone fence. Minny and Abbie slipped silently from their saddles and with a quick hug the former turned and started scaling the rocks, rapidly vanishing into the darkness.

Abbie waited, one hand holding the bridles of both horses, the other resting lightly on the grip of her Pinfire pistol. All was silent apart from the breathing of the two horses, and Abbie felt herself becoming increasingly tense as she waited, expecting the unexpected. Time passed slowly on leaden feet, and still Minny did not return. Night creatures made their nocturnal way around her and on one occasion crawled over her boot prompting her to tense until the creature passed.

Finally when two hours had passed there was a slight scuffling sound above and Minny dropped lightly beside her. Silently the two girls mounted their horses and rode slowly and as quietly as possible back along the trail until they were satisfied that they were out of earshot of any guards at the wall. Then they put their steeds to a canter and rode north to the Eldorado mine.

Arriving at the mine they found that Roger had returned, bringing with him a dozen cavalry troopers who had formed an escort for a party trophy hunting in the foothills of the Rockies. Sitting silently by the campfire with them was their leader, whom Abbie immediately recognized by his fringed buckskin jacket, long moustaches and shoulder-length yellow hair.

But Abbie ignored him, and in concise terms declared that their reconnaissance had been successful. She described the box canyon as being like an elongated U, with the rocky ledge continuing all the way along the left wall to the point where landslides in ages past had created a steep slope from thence to the ground. 'I believe that a night attack on the defence wall could be quite successful, especially if three or four of us worked our way along the ledge and together with a frontal attack employed a goodly quantity of grenades, thus bombing the enemy from above as well as in the main attack!'

There was an excited murmur of approval of Abbie's proposed attack by the assembled men, who finally fell silent when 'Yellow Hair' indolently rose to his feet and advanced upon Abbie. 'Well, well! Quite the little general, aren't you m'dear? What name are we going to call you?'

Coldly Abbie replied, 'My friends call me Abbie, but you can refer to me as Lady Penraven, General!'

General Custer looked suitably abashed, and apologized for his sarcasm.

Looking at him, Abbie nodded silently, 'Right, now shall we complete our plans for the attack?' A detailed discussion followed and Abbie's plan was adopted.

The only opposition came from Custer, who took Roger Gotwald to one side and protested the fact that this 'foreigner' seemed to be giving all the orders, even though she was, after all, only a woman and not a soldier. But Roger clarified the problem for him in the following terms: this was an international situation, in which he, Gotwald, represented the Federal American government, and Lady Penraven represented the British government – and furthermore she had acquired a varied military experience over the years. With those remarks General Custer had to be satisfied.

CHAPTER 12

The next day was spent in final preparations. The remaining bombs were constructed, and all fused with short pieces of tow. Each bomber would carry with him a piece of smouldering tow, or have a burning cigar with which to ignite his grenades. Sacks were found enabling each bomber to carry four or five of the homemade bombs. Juan Garcia was sent to keep an eye on the trail leading to Fort Stroganoff to determine if there was any further activity, and finally, everyone was instructed to try and get some rest before the night's work began.

Time seemed to drag as the long afternoon passed slowly into evening. At last the sun sank beyond the western mountains, and as dusk fell upon the land, the column rode out and made its way to the south-west trail that led to the outlaw fort. In the same grove of aspens used by the girls, they halted and similarly muffled their horses' hoofs, then as the day turned to a moonlit night, they rode silently to the cleft where they were to leave their horses, and where the girls and two young troopers, O'Brien and Devlin, were to ascend to the ledge.

The ledge party had an hour in which to scale the rock face and crawl along the ledge until they were directly above the defence wall. Then after a challenge had been made by the ground party, and if the first bombs had been thrown, they were to set to and hurl and drop theirs until their supply was exhausted. If the situation looked favourable they were then to continue along the ledge, descend behind the house and attempt to force an entry.

Despite the fact that Abbie had swivelled her belt so that her pistol and knife were behind her in order to make it easier for climbing, she still found it a difficult procedure, hanging on to the heavy sack while feeling for hand and footholds. But with whispered encouragement from Minny, and ignoring shoulder muscles screaming with the unaccustomed effort, she finally made it to the ledge where she flopped down, wringing wet with perspiration. There was no time to rest, however, as Trooper O'Brien behind her was gasping for her to pull his sack up on to the ledge, as he was approaching the end of his tether. She did so, and he repeated the process for his fellow soldier, Trooper Devlin.

Then, with Minny in the lead, they worked their way cautiously along the ledge until they were directly above the defence position, lit only by the glowing sparks of cigarettes being smoked by the men on guard duty.

A voice came from out of the darkness. 'Hello, the wall! This is Marshal Frank Thompson speaking. In the name of the United States government, I am ordering you to surrender this position and give yourselves up!' He waited for a reply, which came almost immediately.

'Go to hell, Marshal. We ain't surrendering this place to

anyone, including General Grant!' This defiant response was followed by a flurry of shots from the barricade.

Moments later the first bombs began arriving, having been lobbed over the stone wall by the ground attackers. 'This is our signal!' cried Abbie, standing up and taking from her sack a primed bomb made from a glass jar filled with half a pound of gunpowder in which were mixed some broken glass and old nails. Blowing on the length of smouldering tow she had carried in a small tin, she applied it to the fuse. The fuse sputtered and caught fire, and Abbie hurled the bomb down among the defenders.

Not waiting to see the result of her first bomb, Abbie repeated the operation, as did the other three members of the ledge party, until their supply was exhausted. By that time, the screams for the bombardment to stop were becoming loud and incessant, mingled with cries of 'I surrender!'

Therefore Abbie decided they could well proceed to the second part of the operation, namely the occupation of the fortified house itself.

Edging along the narrow ledge, Abbie obtained a closer look at the building, which was their next objective. Built of squared-off logs with a shingled roof, it looked more like a regular block house than a civilian residence, and this observation was reinforced by the half-a-dozen long guns jutting from the small windows and already spitting death towards the attackers.

As she and her companions moved further towards the end of the canyon the view of the building below naturally changed. There were no windows on the side facing their ledge, and Abbie noted that as the rear came into sight it presented a far less finished appearance, looking more like the rear porch of a ramshackle ranch house with glass-less windows and shutters, now open but which could be closed in adverse weather conditions.

Reaching the scree they slid cautiously down, and with pistols drawn, approached the rear of the log building. A small door, now ajar, gave entry and they went in, glancing quickly into rooms each side of the passageway that led through to the barred front door. On the left was a kitchen with no sign of activity, and on the right an office, where papers strewn on a table and on the floor suggested that some person, or persons, had left in a great hurry. Moving along they encountered yet another doorway on either side of the passageway, and from each came the sound of shots and guttural cries in some foreign tongue of either frustration or failure that they were obviously not stemming the assault.

Abbie and Trooper O'Brien took the left-hand room, and Minny together with Trooper Devlin the one on the right. With pistols cocked, all four jumped through their respective openings, shouting to the occupants to raise their hands. The sudden appearance of attackers from behind stunned most of the riflemen defending the two rooms, and their weapons dropped to the floor as their hands shot in the air. All except for one, who turned to try a shot from the hip at Abbie. She responding with her usual efficiency, and being much faster on the draw, the would-be shooter slumped to the floor clutching a shat-tered shoulder.

O'Brien removed his faded yellow scarf, and tying it to one of the abandoned rifles, waved it to and fro from a window calling out 'Cease fire!' to the ground force attacking the wall. They, meanwhile, had simultaneously been suppressing the last of the resistance of the defenders – and so the action in the box canyon came to a speedy and successful conclusion. Two problems were immediately solved. Mrs Rawlings, the mine owner's wife, was discovered and released unharmed, but unfortunately a grave was found containing the body of McVie, the sheep owner for whom Juan Garcia had worked. He had been taken prisoner, and had been shot while attempting to escape.

Despite all the grenades exploding and the sustained gunfire, casualties were remarkably light. Amongst the defenders two men were killed and fourteen wounded, five from rifle fire, six including the man Abbie had shot in the house, and the remainder injured by bomb fragments. The attackers ended the battle with three men wounded, none being serious injuries.

With the battle over, there were several questions to be answered. First and foremost, where were the three principals who headed the Alaska plot? Information gathered earlier had indicated that they would be found at Fort Stroganoff. The defenders were divided into two separate groups. In one were the men found to be native Russians, pledged to support Stroganoff in his plans. The others were mostly Americans, soldiers of fortune, footloose after the end of the great civil war, and prepared to work for any cause as long as they were paid well.

It was from this latter group that interrogation produced the most information. Stroganoff and his co-conspirators had been in the fort, as an examination of the paperwork in the inner back room would verify, but evidently they had left directly the shooting started. 'How?' demanded Frank Thompson. 'We had this place sown up tight. Nobody could have got out, unless they had wings and flew!'

'I'll tell you Marshal, if you promise to go easy on me!'

Thompson looked around at the other leaders, Gotwald, Abbie and Custer. The latter was still smarting because the plan outlined by a mere female had proven to be so successful. Nobody disagreed. The prisoner offering his services was merely small fry, a pawn in the whole plan, therefore Thompson nodded his grizzled head. 'Very well! You show us how Stroganoff escaped, and I'll see if you can just slip quietly away.'

CHAPTER 13

Mystified, they followed the prisoner into the log dwelling, and through to the room where two of the deputies were busy gathering up and sorting all the paper strewn on the floor and the table. 'Now have your men lift that table to one side and roll up the carpet on which it is sitting.'

They did so, and the bare floor of pine boards revealed a square section about three feet square with a steel ring set in one side. The prisoner pointed to the trap door and explained: 'The house was built over an old mine shaft. That shaft goes down about thirty feet, and then the original owners drove a tunnel horizontally for over four hundred feet with the idea that they were going to reach a mother lode – but it didn't work out that way. They just broke through to another valley, which was tough for them but ideal for Count Stroganoff when he chose this place for his headquarters.'

At a hurried conference certain decisions were made. Custer and his cavalry section were anxious to get back to their hunt camp, and thence back to the regiment at Fort Riley – the General being mollified by Roger Gotwald's statement that his report to William Seward would include a glowing tribute to Custer and his men on the part they played. Therefore they would play no further part in the current affair.

Marshal Thompson and his deputies would have their hands full with the prisoners from both the Eldorado mine and the canyon. Gotwald, upon glancing through some of the papers obtained at the fort and having painfully translated a number of those in Russian, realized that he had to get to San Francisco post haste, where a ship with a cargo of small arms was expected to dock in order to embark Stroganoff bound for Alaska.

That left only Abbie and Minny available to pursue Stroganoff and his associates. Would they be able to do so? Abbie looked over at Minny, who returned the look impassively. 'Well, Roger! Both Minny and I are looking forward to eventually getting back to our home near Colorado City, but we would like to see the end of this hunt, so I guess we will continue.'

Frank Thompson raised a hand. 'There's one small point, Roger. Neither of these two ladies is empowered to legally arrest anyone at this time. I can't do anything about that unless I swear them in as deputies, but I believe you can. Being a Federal representative I think that you can enlist them as fully fledged United States marshals, with powers to detain and arrest anyone suspected of breaking United States law. Why not do so?'

Roger Gotwald stroked his chin in silence for a while, and then said, 'OK, both of you ladies. Each of you raise your right hand. Do you both swear to uphold the constitution of the United States of America and all of its laws,

103

so help you God?' Abbie and Minny were thus legally sworn in, and became badge-carrying deputy US marshals.

The trapdoor was raised and the two girls slowly and cautiously climbed down the ladder mounted against the wall, carefully testing each rung as they went. The way down was lit more clearly by a lantern suspended by a lariat, which was lowered as they descended. Reaching the bottom of the shaft they untied the line, and with the lantern in her left hand and pistol cocked in her right, Abbie, quickly followed by Minny, entered the low subter-ranean tunnel. As they made their way forwards, wondering what denizens of the dark they were likely to encounter, they couldn't help but glance from side to side at the rough-hewn walls, looking dubiously at places sup-ported by rough shoring, very conscious that the whole weight of a mountain was above them. In one part water had collected, but fortunately it came no higher than their ankles, and their riding boots kept their feet dry.

At last the tunnel began to slope upwards, and a faint light ahead indicated that they were nearing the end of their underground journey. The lantern was extinguished, and doubling their caution, the two fledgling marshals crept towards the entrance of the tunnel. This was on the side of a hill and was partially obscured by bushes. Below, on the floor of the valley, was a rough shack with smoke coming from a roof chimney, and off to one side, a corral containing half-a-dozen horses.

One at a time Abbie and Minny crept down the steep slope that led to the shack, making use, as no doubt others had done before them, of the many aspens that caused the pathway to twist and wind as they descended. Eventually they arrived at what was the back wall of the shack, a structure constructed of rough logs notched at the ends and caulked, with moss stuffed between each horizontal member.

Moving around the left corner they crept silently towards the front, where evidently the entrance of the shack was to be found. There was an open window on that side and they crouched down to pass by, but paused as they heard the murmur of two voices within. Listening carefully, Abbie was able to pick up the thread of their conversation.

One voice, in the deep fruity tones of the British aristocracy, was querulously complaining that he did not see why he should have to wait in this God-forsaken spot while his partners were off no doubt enjoying the flesh pots of some local community. 'Dash it, man! How long do they think that I should wait here? It's positively outrageous that I should be acting as a blasted rearguard for a bunch of scoundrels, who have probably made off in some other direction.'

The other male voice, in the rough accent of a plain-speaking American, attempted to placate his companion. 'Well boss, I guess it was just the fact that you were the last man through the tunnel, cos the horses were saddled and ready to leave by the time you finally arrived here.'

'What did they expect!' protested the other. 'First I had to get down that wretched ladder, and I detest heights, then my lantern went out, leaving me in the dark feeling my way along that God-awful passageway. Of course I was late getting here. But I just don't see why they couldn't wait! They are certainly not gentlemen!'

Abbie surmised correctly the speaker was, of course, Sir Bertram Wallace, and he had probably been dumped by his colleagues as so much dead weight, slowing down their own escape, and the story of the rearguard was merely to prevent him following them. She had heard enough.

Sidling around to the front of the shack, followed by Minny, she appeared with pistol drawn in the open doorway. 'Sir Bertram Wallace, I presume! Please get your hands up and place them on top of your head. You too!' This last remark was to the other grey-haired bewhiskered shack occupant, who sat staring at her open mouthed.

Sir Bertram blustered in a quavering voice, 'Who do you think you are, addressing me in that voice? I demand that you put that firearm down at once!'

'I am Lady Abigail Penraven, to you. And currently I am also a deputy United States marshal and I am placing you under arrest.'

Wallace's companion intervened: 'Just do as she says, boss. I don't know anything about those titles she talked about, but she's also the Pinfire Lady and she's deadly if you get her started. I see'd her take on Paul LaRue at Bent's Fort an' she outdrew him completely.'

Bertram Wallace started to comply with Abbie's order, but then changed his mind and made to grab a Tranter handgun that lay upon the table. Abbie hesitated for once, thinking that he might furnish information, but Minny had no such qualms: her Colt .36 Navy barked twice, and Sir Bertram Wallace departed this life to join his ancestors, wherever they might be.

'Thank you, Minny!' Abbie said with a note of frustration in her voice. 'I was hoping to get information from him, but he's no good to me now!'

'Dead man is no good to anyone now!' indicated the ever practical Minny. 'What we do now?'

Abbie turned to the man who had seen her shoot Paul LaRue. 'What do they call you?'

Shaking with fear, being familiar with Abbie's prowess with her Pinfire pistol and no doubt aware that he was in a precarious legal position, 'Whiskers' was reluctant to offer any information. 'W-w-what do you want to know for?'

Abbie regarded him sternly. 'Well, I always like to put a name on a grave, and if I don't get the information I need, that's where you'll be going.'

'Barney's the name! Barney Schmit. I'm telling you the truth, so help me God!' The words came babbling forth from the terrified creature, who was convinced that his last moments were rapidly approaching if he did not tell all that was required.

Stroganoff and Markover had left, telling Barney that, if any more got away through the tunnel, they were to meet at Bailey's Ranch, and together they'd move against what the Russian called 'our secondary target' – but unfortunately Barney had no further details about this. Barney kept stressing that he was just a small cog in a big machine, which Abbie could believe. Bailey's Ranch, Abbie discovered, was developed by one William Bailey about two years previously, and he had built a stagecoach station and also a hotel on the property.

While Abbie extracted information and directions from Barney Schmit, Minny had been selecting horses in the corral. There was only one saddle available, but she assured Abbie that Ute girls were content to ride with just a blanket between them and the horse.

Having furnished Barney with a note describing how he had helped them, and exacting a promise that he would remain at the shack, the two girls rode south-west towards Bailey's Ranch.

CHAPTER 14

Their journey took them south-west through increasingly hilly country with tree-clad slopes on either side. Finally, on the east side of Kenosha Pass, they reached Bailey's Ranch, nestled close to the north fork of the South Platte River.

The two riders halted and surveyed the scene before them. The original ranch building was a simple structure off the trail, in front of which was a single-storey stone building announcing the fact that it was the stage office and relay station. To the right, and actually joined to the station, was a two-storey frame building with an open railed gallery on the upper floor, on which was suspended the sign stating that the edifice was the 'Hotel Excelsior'. The porch of both buildings rested upon a plank board-walk, in front of which was a long hitching rail occupied by several listless horses with drooping heads.

Abbie urged her horse forward, and followed by Minny, rode up to the hotel and dismounted. Two or three men, of the type who seem to be habitually found on hotel porches, looked with curious eyes at the two gun-toting females: Abbie and Minny ignored them, and entered the hotel. Across the rear of the foyer was a counter, behind which a young man sporting a waxed moustache looked at them with great interest.

Ignoring him for a brief moment while she looked the place over, Abbie swiftly determined that to her left was a dining area with a doorway that led into the stage station. To the right of the desk clerk, a stairway led to the upper floor, while behind a glass-fronted partition on her right she heard laughter and the clink of glasses, and correctly surmised that here the hotel bar was to be found.

Advancing to the desk she smiled sweetly at the young man and enquired as to whether there were many guests staying at the hotel, at the same time glancing at the hotel register. Percy Wilson was tongue-tied, staring at this good-looking female looking at him so bewitchingly, yet poised with one hand resting on a heavy pistol.

At length he felt he had to assert his position as a responsible employee of the hotel: 'I, er, don't think I can tell you that, Miss. We don't reveal any information about our guests. Besides which,' he paused and took a deep breath, looking at Minny, 'we don't allow Injuns in here.'

The atmosphere became frosty as Abbie stared at him with hostile eyes. 'Listen, you miserable little pipsqueak. This lady and I are both deputy United States marshals, as can be seen from our badges, and as such, not only can we ask you questions and expect answers, but we can also legally close this establishment if the answers are not forthcoming. Do I make myself clear?'

Startled by the abrupt change that he had evoked in the young woman before him, Percy made haste to give her the information she sought. 'There's a drummer, name of Crowe, in the bar. He arrived two days ago. There's a religious man, the Reverend Benjamin Allgood, and Elsie his daughter.' He smirked, 'They're upstairs. There's a couple of mining men, Ed Budchek and Bob Wells: they've been here a week, drinking steadily in the bar. Then there's two gentlemen that arrived today. One said he's from New York, the other's a foreign gentleman. Don't know yet whether they're staying or just passing through. They met a couple of strangers here, and went into the bar.' Eager to make amends Percy said ingratiatingly, 'I trust that is satisfactory, Marshal?'

Abbie gave him a nod, and motioned for him to stay behind his counter, then she and Minny made their way over to the bat-wing doors screening the bar.

Listening to the discourse within, she smiled and pushed open the doors, stepping in quickly, followed by Minny. Their entry into this all-male domain created a frozen tableau, during which James Crowe continued to hold aloft a pair of lady's pink drawers, identical to, or the facsimile thereof, of the garment he had flourished during the stagecoach journey. His salesman's patter had meanwhile come to a sudden stop as he stared at the pair standing in the doorway, followed by an ejaculation of, 'The Pinfire Lady, by all that's wonderful. And that's her Indian companion, Minny.'

'Jim Crowe! Still peddling ladies' underwear I see!' declared Abbie, who swiftly observed the other men seated at the large round table with Crowe. One, by his style of dress and general appearance, she believed was Stroganoff, and to his right, wearing the sobre attire of a

111

New York businessman, was undoubtedly Hiram P. Markover. The other table occupant with his back to her was unknown, but from what she could see of the way he wore a low-slung pistol belt, he appeared to be a gun-fighter. There was also one empty chair whose owner, another gunfighter, was just turning away from the bar. Her lightning glance took in several other men, miners from their rough apparel, nursing drinks at the bar or being served by a typical white-aproned barman adorned with a bushy moustache who stood poised with both hands on the counter top.

He was the first to break the silence. 'Sorry ladies, you can't come in here! There's no women allowed! Besides which . . .' he paused, looking at Minny, 'that gal is most certainly not white, and it's against the law to serve liquor to Indians. You know that!'

Abbie responded with a harsh tone in her voice. 'Then you have a big problem, little man, because she is the Law. We are both duly sworn in deputy United States marshals, and I hereby order that you all remain here, and also get your hands away from your guns!' This last remark was to the seated gunfighter, whose right hand was moving slowly, as she spoke, towards his holster.

While Minny remained by the doorway, alert for any adverse moves, Abbie advanced to the table looking searchingly at the four seated men. She grinned at Jim Crowe, still holding his pink sales sample, and relieved the tension somewhat by indicating that he could put his underwear away . . . slowly.

Abbie then turned to the Russian, and relying on the fact that she knew that he had a title, she deliberately addressed him as; 'Mr Nikolai Stroganoff, I presume?'

Stroganoff stiffened in his chair. His eyes glared at this impertinent young woman who dared to address him thus, and speaking through gritted teeth, he replied, 'Young woman, my name is Count Stroganoff and you will address me properly! In Russia I would have you whipped for daring to insult me!'

Before Abbie could respond, the situation exploded. In the doorway a deep booming voice exclaimed, 'What's going on here?' Startled, Abbie chanced a glance in that direction, and saw a stout, white-haired fellow with a clerical collar standing there flourishing a Remington .44 calibre revolver. Beside him and slightly to the left was a young, attractive-looking girl, feverishly trying to load a .32 calibre tip-up Smith & Wesson.

The unknown gunman seated at the table seized the opportunity caused by the diversion at the door to grab the pink drawers from Jim Crowe, and throw them at Abbie, causing her further distraction. But used to working together as a team, the two marshals reacted instantly: Minny, standing beside the doorway, drew her .36 Navy Colt and shot the reverend gentleman in the arm that was raising his pistol and, for good measure, once in the lower abdomen. As his gun dropped to the floor, his fair young 'daughter' squealed with terror, and dropping the partially loaded cylinder of her 'tip-up', fled from the scene.

Meanwhile, Abbie had dropped to a crouch as she drew her 12mm Pinfire and triggered two shots at the unknown thrower of feminine garments. He had drawn and in fact fired first, but the shot from his .44 Colt went over Abbie's head, since she was rapidly changing position. Her two shots did not miss, but the first was far from lethal, merely removing a large portion of his left ear, while the second tore a nasty furrow the length of his right arm.

Sensing activity to her right, Abbie swung in that direction and chanced a snap shot at the second gunfighter, the ball catching him in the throat and, as later deduced, tearing through the trachea and breaking his spinal column, thus ending his existence.

The rest of the bar's patrons had scattered to safety when the gun-play began. Some dived for the floor, but most stampeded for the doorway, suddenly having urgent business elsewhere. Seizing his chance as Abbie was rendering the gunman by the bar speechless, Stroganoff jumped to his feet and, ignoring his American colleague, scuttled from the room – accompanied by his bloody-eared associate, he fled on horseback.

Markover, seeing himself thus abandoned, decided at this late hour to play a hand in the game. He drew a Derringer from an inside pocket and aimed it at Abbie's back as she dealt with the gunman by the bar. As he did so, he received a blow in the chest, followed by yet another fatal pounding, which effectively ended his earthly career. His last vision as his eyes clouded over was that of the contemptible garment salesman standing there holding a heavy .41 calibre revolver with two hands.

Abbie, who had seen the last activity out of the corner of an eye, was as usual quick to express her thanks at the salesman's intervention. 'Thank you, Mr Crowe! Those two shots were most timely. What have you got there? It looks quite formidable compared with that little S&W that you carried on the stagecoach.'

'It's an English gun. I took it in trade. They call it a Webley Bentley. I understand that the Rebels used them during the war. The fella I got it from had been in the Union army, so I guess he took it from some Johnny Reb. Then, when he desperately wanted some articles to impress his gal, he traded it. I'm glad that he did.'

'So am I, Mr Crowe! So am I!' replied Abbie with a smile.

The acrid smoke in the bar room gradually cleared as Abbie issued fresh orders. The dead bodies of Markover and the unknown gunmen were to be searched before being removed for burial. Someone was sent to bring the local vet, who, in lieu of a medical doctor, could possibly attend to the wounded Reverend Allgood, whose wound, though embarrassing, was unlikely to be fatal. And Minnie was dispatched to unearth Elsie, the wounded one's 'daughter'.

In a very short time Abbie's instructions were carried out. The two bodies were diligently searched, the contents of their pockets forming a small pile on the round table, before being carted away to a nearby stable, there to await burial in the local Boot Hill. The vet arrived and, chuckling, proceeded to a swift examination of the groaning figure lying on the floor, hands clutching his nether regions.

Eventually, a grinning Minny arrived, shepherding at gun point a terrified, red-eyed Elsie, still snivelling, as she twisted and tore a lace handkerchief to shreds. Abbie looked at her companion enquiringly.

'She play hide and seek with me. I find her under bed.

She no want to come out, so I talk nicely. Then she come!'

Abbie smiled at Minny's wide definition of the word 'nicely', and motioned for Elsie to be seated.

Indicating that the girl should tell her story, Abbie listened between sobs to a tale as old as the hills. Elsie Sumers had been born and raised on a farm in the state of Illinois. She was sixteen years old and was dissatisfied with her lot in life. Reading an advertisement in a local paper that entertainers were wanted in Oro City Colorado, this unsophisticated country girl had answered the advertisement and, receiving a polite letter of welcome and a stagecoach voucher, had slipped away from home without telling her parents and made her way westward. To her horror, her journey had ended with her being deposited in a bordello run by Sally Purple, a notorious, hard-faced madam, who claimed that Elsie could not leave until she had paid back the debts of stagecoach, meals and accommodation accumulated on her behalf.

This Elsie had been doing unwillingly, and then the Reverend Allgood had turned up and promised to get her away from the sordid life she was living. He had succeeded in persuading her (and paid a handsome price to Madam, surmised Abbie to herself), but she found that she had gone from the fat to the fire as his Reverence expected her to be his constant bed companion.

Abbie pressed her for information as to why they had come to Bailey's Ranch, but all Elsie knew was that they had met the Russian, and she was told that they would be coming into a lot of money. Then her owner, for so he described himself, had given her the S&W and briefly demonstrated how to load it, just before the ruckus started in the bar downstairs.

Abbie pondered about Elsie being so uninformed, but apart from riding willy-nilly after Stroganoff, she did not know what to do, as she was in ignorance as to his next move. She shrugged her shoulders philosophically, and thought 'Ah well, two down and one to go, it could be worse.' She went through the items deposited on the table: a deck of playing cards, three 20-dollar gold pieces and some small change, a handsome watch, a clasp knife, and a small circular tin container of percussion caps – this was the sorry total of two men's lives. There was nothing else.

She turned to Elsie. 'Are you sure that there was nothing else? Think, girl!'

Elsie shook her head violently, 'No ma'am, I've told you the honest truth. He just said we were going to be rich with a lucky strike. An' he laughed like he was mighty contented. That's all! Honest!'

Abbie walked up and down, pensively repeating Elsie's last words to her – and then it hit her like a ton of bricks. *Lucky strike!* Of course, she herself was the owner of the Lucky Strike gold mine, west of Colorado City. It could be that Stroganoff and a reinforced gang intended to hit the mine and then head west towards the Pacific coast. It was guesswork, but Abbie was sure that she was correct.

'Minny! Find us fresh horses and a pack animal to carry supplies. Percy!' She roared. And the quavering desk clerk arrived, anxious to amend the previous impression of non-cooperation that he had created. 'Percy, I want a pack horse, and supplies for two – bacon, flour, beans, coffee and vegetables, dehydrated if you've got any. And get it out here sacked and packed ready to go in no more than an hour. Jump to it, Percy!' And the desk clerk scurried away, desperate to please, but also to get rid of the pistol-waving marshal who had just killed two men.

Abbie picked up the three gold pieces from the table. 'Elsie, I want you to take this money and use it to go home. Don't tell the whole story if you don't want to. Just that you made a big mistake and you are sorry. Now promise that you'll do as I say!'

Elsie whispered a fervent promise as she clutched the money in her fist and then, with a sob, threw herself into Abbie's arms, crying with happiness. Abbie, uncomfortable with these displays of affection, patted her awkwardly on the shoulder several times while muttering what she hoped were words of encouragement, before pushing her away and turning to examine the work of the veterinarian.

Benjamin Allgood would probably survive, although it was highly possible that he would have to live a celibate life in the future. A search of his pockets revealed little of interest except for a note, presumably from Stroganoff or one of his confederates, arranging a meeting at Bailey's Ranch. His clerical attire was obviously a sham, and his real vocation was displayed by a marked deck of cards and a pair of loaded dice. Abbie finished her examination as Minny returned with the news that all was ready at the hitching rail; then with a final nod to Elsie, the two marshals left the hotel.

Climbing into the saddle, Abbie noted with pleasure the addition of a Henry lever-action rifle resting in a sheath. Noting a second piece adorning the latter's rig, she asked 'Where on earth did you get these from, Minny?'

'Guns in room of Holy Man, Abbie! I figure he not need them any more. I borrow them. Is OK Abbie?'

Abbie smiled at her Ute friend and nodded, 'Is certainly OK, Minny! Let's go!' and she urged her horse into a trot with Minny following, leading the pack animal.

CHAPTER 15

Despite an auspicious start it wasn't long before the journey south turned into an unmitigated disaster. They had been on the trail for close on two hours and a decision was made to save time by cutting across country and thereby avoid all the winds and twists of the route chosen more for wheeled traffic than for those on horseback.

All went well until the pack animal stepped into a grass-concealed gopher hole. There was an ominous crack and the poor beast stood there on three good legs with the fourth raised in pain and a piteous look on its face as though it knew what was going to happen.

Abbie and Minny looked at each other in dismay, and after a few choice comments, proceeded to unpack the load and distribute the essentials between their remaining two animals. Of necessity, some items had to be abandoned, but finally they were finished and their pack horse stood there patiently awaiting its inevitable end. There was a pause. The two girls looked at each other, and eventually Abbie shrugged her shoulders, drew her Pinfire revolver and, standing closer, fired a bullet into the injured horse's left ear, killing the animal instantly.

Without a word they both mounted and rode quickly from the scene, anxious to make up the lost time. But within the next hour Abbie noticed the gait of her horse was becoming uneven, and getting worse with every step. She halted, and dismounting, checked every hoof, and soon found that one of the hind shoes was irreparably loose. The only solution was to remove the offending shoe, then climb up behind Minny and, leading her horse, continue their trek until they could find a blacksmith.

Back on the southward trail once more it was with great relief that Abbie saw a hand-painted sign on a a piece of board tacked to a post at the side of the rutted pathway: 'Colorado Springs, 2 miles'. Minny urged her weary roan forward.

Entering the built-up area that constituted the city limits, they rode along the unpaved main street looking for a smithy, ignoring the many curious glances cast in their direction. 'I suppose it is a trifle strange to see two people on one horse, especially if the two are women,' said Abbie to herself as they sought their objective. A sign announcing 'J. Wulfson, Blacksmith', and the sound of metal striking metal on an anvil beyond a wide open doorway, found them what they required.

They dismounted, and tethering their steeds to a post in lieu of a rail, entered the smithy. The blacksmith was hard at work, wielding a heavy hammer in one hand while holding a red-hot piece of iron with long tongs in the other, beating the metal into shape on the anvil. He paused, quenching the new horseshoe by plunging it into a drum of water. Then, and only then, did the smith, a black-bearded giant wearing a leather apron and a shirt speckled with tiny burn marks, turn in their general direction and enquire, 'Yes, ladies? How can I be of assistance to you?'

Before Abbie could respond stating their requirements, there was a violent interruption: 'You two gals, freeze! This is the sheriff speaking!' They turned their heads and saw that they were being menaced by three men armed with sawn-off shotguns. 'Now raise your hands above your heads, slowly, and then don't move a muscle!'

A fourth man entered the smithy and, moving clear of the shotguns, walked behind the girls and swiftly relieved them of their pistols and knives. Once they had been disarmed they were permitted to lower their hands with the warning; 'No tricks, now! One false move and you'll get a blast from these greeners!'

In vain Abbie protested that both she and Minny were lawfully authorized US marshals in pursuit of criminals, and furthermore, as the Pinfire Lady she was known far and wide in Colorado and indeed throughout the West. The sheriff, tight-lipped, refused to listen to Abbie's protestations, and the two girls were hustled from the smithy and down the street, past jeering onlookers, to his office where they had the mortification of hearing a cell door clang shut as they were locked in.

Finally, when the sheriff had completed sundry other tasks and ostensibly tidied up the papers on his desk, he released Abbie, but not Minny, and permitted her to sit while he fired questions at her. Abbie submitted to this verbal barrage for a few minutes, and then slammed a small fist down on his scarred desktop, at the same time shouting:

'Be quiet and listen to me for a change! You have arrested two officers of the law at gunpoint presumably on nothing but a whim! First of all, perhaps you would explain the reasons for your action?'

'Well, the gentleman who said you would be coming this way was a US marshal himself. Said he was in pursuit of a gang of criminals, and that you two were part of the gang and were determined to stop him doing his duty. He was well dressed, and spoke like an educated man but with a slight foreign accent, like many Americans these days. He had papers with him. There was no reason to doubt his credentials.'

Abbie was so exasperated she could not contain herself. 'You gullible fool! Don't you realize what you've done? That man is no US marshal, he's Count Stroganoff, a Russian bent on conspiring against the United States and, incidentally against Great Britain. You may have created an international incident!'

By this time the sheriff was having serious misgivings about the arrest of these two women, but being a stubborn man, he was not prepared to surrender his position. He stroked his chin and pulled at his long droopy moustache before replying; 'Well, there may be something in what you say, but it certainly sounds like a far-fetched fairytale to me, woman. How are you going to prove it?'

'Look! You could send a rider to my ranch, the Pinfire, outside Colorado City, and get confirmation, or you could send your men around the stores here asking if anyone here can identify the person known as the Pinfire Lady. That might prove to be the quickest way – but whichever, do something!'

123

More time elapsed while Sheriff Marsden slowly pondered over the recent conversation that he'd had with the fair prisoner before him. Meanwhile Abbie sat, outwardly calm but inwardly fuming at this officer of the law whose thought processes seemed as slow as molasses in January.

Finally he stirred, returned Abbie to her cell, and going to the door of the office sent two of the deputies on a search to see if anyone in town could identify the person calling herself the Pinfire Lady. Meanwhile in the cell, Minny, with the stoicism of her tribe, sat cross-legged motionless on a bunk, while Abbie, frustrated, paced up and down like a caged lioness.

Time passed slowly, and to Abbie, glancing periodically at the large clock on the wall of the office, it appeared that the large hand was completely motionless. The light faded as the afternoon sun sank down behind the mountains, and the sheriff lit an oil lamp in the office.

Finally, one of the deputies returned with the news that the other was coming, bringing with him a woman who just had to close up her store first. Eventually, footsteps were heard approaching on the boardwalk, followed by the sound of a man and a woman in conversation. The door opened, and a middle-aged woman entered, followed by the other deputy. 'You wanted to see me, sheriff?'

Then, glancing towards the cell door, she gasped: 'Abbie Penraven, by thunder! What on earth are you doing in there, captain?' addressing Abbie with the title she had employed when commanding the wagon train. Turning back to the stupefied official seated at his desk, she demanded, 'What tomfoolery have you been up to now, Bert Marsden? That lady that you've got in that there cell is Lady Penraven, the Pinfire Lady. An' she saved my life and the lives of several people a few years back. Besides which she is, or was, one of the fastest guns in this neck of the woods. An' you've got the gall to lock her up like a common criminal?'

Abbie stood there relieved at the identification given by this unknown person – and then suddenly she recognized her: 'Ann Marlowe! Am I sure glad to see you!' And the two old friends stood exchanging news and reminiscing about their first meeting west of the hamlet of Paradise in Kansas.

In vain Sheriff Marsden attempted to re-establish his authority, to the amusement of the two deputies present. Finally, he gave up and surrendered himself to the situation at hand. Unlocking the cell door he said plaintively, 'Ann! Would you please get your friends out of here! I'm sorry! A mistake has been made and I just hope that you ladies won't hold it against me!'

Abbie, now that she and Minny had their freedom, was anxious to hit the trail. But it was not to be. Because of the arrests, the blacksmith, rather than shoeing their horses, had merely turned the animals into a corral; therefore time was wasted securing both horses, rounding up the smith from his favourite saloon, then waiting while he re-ignited the furnace and finally shod both horses.

Since there was nothing to be done until the smith had completed his work, Abbie, Minny and Ann Marlowe repaired to a local eatery, where they were treated to a satisfactory meal paid for by the truly penitent sheriff, who had one eye on the next election, and could see his chances of retaining his seat rapidly diminishing if Ann spread the word of how he had made a fool of himself.

Abbie enjoyed the meal and the companionship, but was anxious to get going regardless of the hour. Therefore she was greatly relieved when a small boy appeared with the news that their horses were finally shod, saddled and ready. There were no charges to be paid, the sheriff had seen to that. Bidding farewell to Ann with the usual mutual vows to keep in touch, Abbie and Minny, thankful that it was a moonlit and starlit night, finally resumed the pursuit.

CHAPTER 16

For a pleasant change the next few days were uneventful as they pressed south into more familiar territory. Reaching the approximate longitude of Colorado City, they swung west, deliberately avoiding the town and heading straight for the Pinfire Ranch, arriving shortly after six o'clock when normally, folks in both the cook-house and ranch would be sitting down enjoying their evening meal. Today, however, tranquillity was absent and turmoil had taken its place, with people running hither and thither or riding up on unknown tasks, directed by a stocky figure standing on the ranch-house porch.

Approaching closer, the director of the commotion could be seen to be the person of Jack Harding, the ranch foreman, who stared, momentarily puzzled by the arrival of the two riders; then with a single cry of 'Abbie!', he jumped down the porch steps with a single bound and came running towards them. Reaching them he literally pulled Abbie from the saddle, hugging her effusively, at the same time crying, 'Look people, the Pinfire Lady is back, it's a bloomin' miracle! That's what it is. A bloomin' miracle! Dora! Dora! Look 'oo's 'ere!'

Jack continued to call out until Dora, his wife, accompanied by the diminutive figures of a little boy and his sister, came down the steps to greet the newcomers, Dora with cries of joy, the children more restrained, being uncertain as to what all the commotion was about.

Other people came up and the excitement rose until Abbie felt it was time to bring all down to a sober level. 'Quiet people, please! Both Minny and I are extremely happy to see everyone, but I can tell from the way Jack was acting when we arrived that something is amiss. So perhaps you will all give us a short while for Jack to make his report before you celebrate our return. Minny, will you take care of the horses and then join us in the ranch house?'

Minny did as requested, and Abbie, Jack, Dora and the two children walked over to the ranch building and entered the commodious living room, then settled down to hear the foreman's report.

Jack, in his ponderous English way, started to deliver a full report of all the activities that had occurred during Abbie's nigh-on two-year absence, but she cut him off with a wave of her hand, 'Don't bother about all that, Jack. I'm sure that all problems have been handled with your usual efficiency. Tell me about the attack on the gold mine. That is the cause of all the commotion, is it not?'

Jack's jaw dropped open in amazement at Abbie's words: ''Ow in the name of all that's 'oly, did you 'ear about that?'

Abbie quickly gave him an abbreviated account of all that had occurred during her return from England, dwelling on her pursuit of Nikolai Stroganoff, and the way in which she and Minny had thwarted the Russian's plans. 'After our last encounter at Bailey's Ranch, we discovered that he intended to rob a gold mine to further his plans, and the phrase "Lucky Strike" made us believe that *our* mine was the target. And I'm presuming that our surmise was correct. Now, Jack! Your story, if you please.'

Jack Harding scratched his head and attempted to get his thoughts in order; 'Well Abbie, you know that I've always liked a steady routine. A leftover from the army days, I guess. After we got the smelter installed three years ago, we tried to vary as much as possible the times when we were shipping bullion. Earlier, when we shipped ore, it was a far less attractive target, but gold bars draw the criminals like bees to a honey pot.

'So, as I say, rather than ship the gold always at the same time, I've tried to vary the dates, and even the hours of departure.'

Abbie interrupted him; 'Jack Harding! Tell me exactly what happened! Stop flannelling around, to use one of your famous army expressions. Get to the point, man!'

'Sorry, Abbie!' He took a deep breath. 'Well, yesterday, up at the mine, all was evidently as usual, with nothing out of the ordinary. A shipment of gold, 'bout 40,000 dollars in value, was sitting boxed in the strongroom ready to go directly I gave the word. A party of men rode up, dressed in Federal army uniform, and stated that they had instructions to escort the gold to Santa Fe. Bill Travis, the overseer, was suspicious from the start – you know what he's like – and demanded to see their paperwork, and especially the authorization to move the gold. That's when things got nasty.

'The officer drew a pistol and shot 'im! Not fatally, but deliberately in order to obtain the combination for the lock of the strongroom. Bill deliberately fainted, and so, since that approach didn't work, they broke into the powder store and blew the door to get at the gold. Then they departed, after leaving the workers crowded together in a locked room. Hours later, Bill managed to recover enough to free the men and sent word to me about the raid. Abbie, I 'ate to say it, but I think they had inside information!'

'What exactly do you mean, Jack? Elaborate!'

'Well, about three months ago Bill hired a fella, name of Henry Ketchum, as a general labourer. We were a bit short-handed due to sickness. This chap had a varied past – soldier, cowboy, bouncer in a bar, and a stagecoach guard. He had a distinctive scar on his face which gave him a scowl, but Bill and I both thought that he'd prove useful, and he appeared clean, so we hired him. His work was satisfactory, but then one day I found him here rifling through the office papers. I gave him a right bawling out, and he took off for the city an' hasn't been back since.'

'I presume you mean Colorado City, Jack?' Her foreman nodded, and Abbie turned to Minny, who had silently entered the room earlier.

'Sorry Min'! I'm going to need a horse saddled again. You haven't seen your folks for quite a while, so if you'd rather stay here and visit with them, I quite understand.'

'You make silly talk, Abbie! Where you go, Minny always there too! I go saddle two horses!'

Meanwhile Abbie extracted a detailed description of

Henry Ketchum's appearance, with the added information that when he wasn't working, he had spent his time practising with his six gun, an 1860 model .44 Colt.

The two pals rode over to Colorado City, Abbie noting with concern that the town had not grown much during her absence. It still presented the same view of unpainted shacks, sod-roofed log cabins and the same number of false-fronted clapboard buildings joined by an uneven boardwalk. Benson was still operating the general store, but Abbie continued along the rut-filled street, finally halting in front of the Bonanza saloon, still managed, she understood, by Bobby Smith and his mother.

'Young Bobby can't still be "young" now,' thought Abbie to herself, as she and Minny dismounted; after hitching their horses' reins at the rail, they strode across the boardwalk, nodding to the idlers seated as usual on the porch, and paused at the bat-wing doors of the saloon.

Being mid-evening by this time a fair number of patrons were present, some standing nursing their drinks at the bar, while others sat either engaged in quiet discussion at the small circular tables dotted around, or tried their luck with the Faro dealer seated in the corner.

Abbie recognized a good number of those present as being locals from the town or from the surrounding area. Several, from their dress, she spotted as being from the mine. One man, however, sat alone, staring morosely into a shot glass with a half-filled bottle of whiskey at his left elbow. She noticed that he answered the description Jack Harding had given her of Henry Ketchum, and observed that fellow patrons passing by gave him a wide berth.

Pushing on the bat-wing doors, Abbie and Minny went

into the saloon. The entry of two women into what was considered a male domain caused the desultory conversations to cease as the newcomers walked up to Ketchum's table.

'Mr Ketchum! My name is Abbie Penraven. I am the owner of the Lucky Strike mine, among other things, and I would like to have a little talk with you!'

Ketchum stared up at her with hard, insolent eyes and tossed back his glass of liquor. 'I've got nothing to say to you, lady. I don't care if you're the Queen of Sheba! Go to hell!' and he deliberately ignored Abbie as he poured more whiskey into his shot glass.

As he raised it to his lips Abbie stepped forwards and with her left hand knocked the glass from his hand, spilling the contents over him, the table and the floor. Simultaneously, her right hand swept down and drew her Pinfire revolver, cocking the piece and jamming the muzzle between his startled eyes.

'One move and you're dead meat, mister! I want a little talk with you, and I want it now!' and to emphasize her demand she pushed a little harder on her pistol, forcing Ketchum's head back at an unnatural angle.

Minny had swiftly moved around to the rear of Ketchum's seat and deftly removed his pistol and also an ugly-looking knife. She searched him expertly and nodding to Abbie muttered, 'Him OK, Abbie. Be a good boy now,' and she patted his shoulder, oblivious of the rage building in the would-be gunman at just being disarmed by two females.

Abbie re-holstered her revolver, and lightly folding her arms, stared down at Henry Ketchum, saying:

'Now that we've drawn your fangs, perhaps we can have the little talk that I mentioned. Now, Mr Ketchum, you were working at the Lucky Strike and you suddenly ceased to come to your place of employment. Curiously, you never bothered to pick up your last week's pay, either. That is very strange, since I hear that you were trying to borrow a few dollars the previous week, telling people that you were short of cash. Yet here we find you sitting drinking, with a near full bottle of whiskey in front of you. Doesn't that strike you as needing an explanation?'

Abbie's last question was addressed not only to Henry Ketchum, but also to the bar patrons at large, as she wanted to enlist their support in obtaining information regarding the gold theft, which affected the whole community.

Acting on a sudden thought Abbie requested assistance from those present. 'While Minny and I keep Mr Ketchum covered, would two of you gentlemen search him thoroughly? From head to toe please!'

Two of the miners present volunteered. Ketchum reluctantly rose under the persuasion of both Abbie's and Minny's revolvers, and the two searchers did a thorough job, emptying the suspect's pockets and leaving them inside out while the contents were placed on the table. The rewards of their search were quite interesting, and included a silver pocket watch, a small penknife, an envelope and some folded paper, several Federal bills amounting to eighteen dollars, some small change and four twenty-dollar gold pieces.

A muttered growl emerged from the onlookers, as it became increasingly obvious that Henry Ketchum was a man who quite possibly could have placed their own employment in jeopardy. Abbie motioned for the two miners to stand clear, and addressed herself to Ketchum: 'Perhaps you would care to explain where you obtained the gold coins lying on the table?'

Sullenly he shook his head, 'I ain't saying anything!'

Abbie tried again, pointing out the fact that Ketchum was facing a long term of imprisonment if his involvement in the gold robbery was proven in a court of law, whereas by cooperating, the act would certainly stand in his favour.

'Le' me think for a minute,' he said, rubbing his bristled chin with his left hand and glancing around the room as though seeking allies, or possibly weighing up his chances.

Minny was to his left, and as he turned in her direction, his left leg buckled as though he suddenly stumbled, and he lunged against her, seizing her Colt and pushing her violently away with his left hand. Ketchum was thumbing back the hammer for a snap shot at Abbie as the latter drew her Pinfire revolver, and both fired almost simultaneously, with the sound of his shot sounding like an echo of hers.

Henry Ketchum's shot tugged at the side of Abbie's buckskin shirt as it sped past to embed itself in the doorpost of the saloon. Abbie's shot, with her usual deadly accuracy, smashed into his chest, followed by the habitual second one, with scarcely two inches between the two holes. Ketchum was driven backwards and fell to the ground lifeless, with Minny's pistol dropping from his open hand.

There was a momentary stunned silence as Abbie stood

there poised, her revolver held rock steady in both hands, tendrils of grey smoke curling up from the muzzle as she waited for any sign that her latest opponent might recover and resume the fight. Then a hubbub of noise broke out as bar patrons sought to make sense of the gunfight they had just experienced.

Abbie holstered her pistol and sank into a chair. 'Phew, that was close! Minny, are you OK?'

Minny had retrieved her pistol from the floor, and after examining it, thrust it almost angrily into the holster.

'Sorry Abbie! I think Ketchum man OK, as have no gun. I no think he rustle my Colt!'

'Don't worry about it, Minny. Sit down while I go through Ketchum's paperwork.' And Abbie proceeded to examine closely the late Ketchum's envelope and paper lying on the table.

The envelope was but a sad indictment of the man's character, being a plea from a young girl, Isabel, dismissed from her position working with a family due to the discovery that she was expecting a child, and would 'dear Henry' do the right thing and return and marry her.

Bobby Smith was reading the letter over Abbie's shoulder and made a comment regarding Ketchum's character, whereupon Abbie decided to utilize the saloon manager as a one-time secretary.

'Bobby! I need to use your services. This letter has a return address. I want you to compose a little letter to Isabel explaining that Henry has met with a fatal accident, and get the four gold pieces to her. The balance can be used to pay the undertaker for his burial.'

Abbie then turned to the folded sheets of paper found

135

upon searching Ketchum. Smoothing them out on the table, the first contained ample evidence of Ketchum's treachery. It showed a detailed map of the Lucky Strike mine, emphasizing the strongroom and the powder store. Presumably the map was a copy, the original being used by the raiders. Heaven knows why Ketchum had hung on to the copy, unless it was vanity, although he may have had ideas about a second raid.

The second sheet was a set of instructions laid out specifically for Ketchum, detailing that, after the raid, he was to remain in the Colorado City area for a full week in case Hiram Markover should succeed in escaping from Bailey's Ranch. At the end of that time, with or without the American financier, he was to ride west and link up with Stroganoff at Salt Lake City and thence to San Francisco, California.

Abbie considered their options. Fortunately Stroganoff, being a methodical man, had spelled out the complete details of his campaign, and therefore it was merely a question of reacting successfully to his intended plan. Roger Gotwald, the Federal agent, was hopefully already in or on his way to San Francisco, and he could enlist additional aid there. That would plug one bolt hole. Should she ride to cut off Stroganoff's trail between Colorado City and Salt Lake, or should she ride post haste for the Mormon capital and hope to be able to intercept him and his gang upon their arrival?

Having pondered the options, Abbie decided on the latter course of action. Sending a note to Jack Harding for him to select four volunteers to catch up with her and Minny with pack horses and supplies, she and her Ute friend, together with two braves from the latter's tribe, headed westwards, hoping to pick up the trail of the gold-mine bandits.

CHAPTER 17

Abbie's idea, after examining a map of the western United States as then known, was to head due west as the terrain allowed, until they could reach the Old Spanish Trail which curved north-west through south-west Colorado into Utah, continuing north in that territory until about fifty miles south of Salt Lake City, before swinging south-west and heading for Los Angeles on the California coast.

She tried hard to put herself in the frame of mind possessed by Stroganoff and his gold bandits. His pack train of horses or mules heavily laden with boxes of gold bars would not travel too far each day for fear of taxing the animals too much, thereby creating a situation where their animals were dying on them. Therefore it should be possible to get ahead of them.

Another aspect that Stroganoff quite possibly had not considered when selecting his route of escape was the unsettled environment apparently existing in Utah Territory. Since Salt Lake City had become the headquarters of the Mormons, a religion disliked and feared in many of the eastern areas of the United States, the whole of Utah Territory had been in a state of turmoil, with stories of bands of 'gentiles' (non-Mormons) being harassed and even massacred in their travels west. There were tales of women being carried off to become 'hidden' wives of male Mormons, practising their desire for polygamy, and apparently a semi-state of war existed between some elements of Mormonism and the United States army units sent to keep peace and administer the law in the territory.

It was Abbie's hope that they could have a confrontation with Stroganoff before entering Utah territory, where there would be the added problem of possible religious strife, for she personally had no desire to become a wife, hidden or otherwise!

Each day as they headed westward the terrain grew more rugged, with towering cliffs and jagged peaks on either side. This was where the Ute braves were invaluable, roaming far ahead of the main party, scouting out routes which enabled the latter to keep forging forwards, when by their own efforts they would have had to continually backtrack when selected trails became impassable.

As they travelled they sought word of any pack trains heading west, or of any westward-bound parties led by a man with a foreign accent. From many queries in isolated settlements, and even from single shepherds and cattlemen, they managed to glean slender slivers of information, and gradually developed a picture of their quarry.

Stroganoff was having problems in several ways. A number of the men that he had recruited were apparently complaining about the way in which he lorded it over them, treating them more like Russian serfs rather than free-borne Americans, even threatening to use a knout on them. His commissariat plans had obviously gone awry, since he had been supplementing his limited stocks by attempting to purchase food at isolated trading posts on their route. And one of the muleskinners that he had hired had attempted to desert and had been promptly shot.

The foregoing were just some of Stroganoff's little problems. The main issue confronting him was his choice of animals. Ignoring the advice of men familiar with handling mules, he had bought a number of animals that were barefoot – that is, they were unshod, being hitherto employed in field use. On the rocky trails carrying heavy loads they soon broke down.

Upon hearing this Sam Brewer, a lanky, brown-faced, forty-year-old man who hailed from Alabama, burst into a storm of laughter. 'Haw, haw!' he chuckled, 'It's the Jackass Brigade all over again!'

Upon being asked to explain his merriment, Sam said, 'Well, Miss Abbie, during the late war the Yankees sent a raiding column down into 'Bama. They gathered up for government service over a thousand mules, all barefooted critters, and they soon began to break down. With all those mules a-braying at night-time, getting loose and stampeding all over the countryside, 'Bama countryfolk soon christened them the "Jackass Brigade". Ole Bedford Forrest, he hassled that Yankee column as they staggered on with those poor young mules giving out due to sore backs and tender hoofs until, finally, he tricked them blue-bellies into believing that he had twice as many men as they did, and that he had them surrounded. Actually, he had only half the strength of that Yankee column, but they surrendered anyway. That's why I was a-laughing, ma'am, cos I figure ole Stroganoff has got himself into a similar situation!'

While Sam Brewer was the centre of attention with his Civil War tale of the barefoot mules, Minny was whispering animatedly with the two Ute braves, and as Sam brought his story to a close, she grabbed one of the two by the elbow and half dragged him forwards. Muttering to him in the Ute tongue, she then reverted to English saying, 'White Buffalo has important words to say, Abbie. He no speak much white eyes' language, but I tell you what he say,' and she poked him in the side urgently.

White Buffalo looked down at her and said something in a very low voice which Abbie surmised was probably in the nature of 'Stop nagging me, woman! I'm getting ready to speak!'

Then folding his arms and adopting a heroic stance, he launched into a speech as though he were running for Congress. The other brave remained impassive, apart from the odd 'Huh!' apparently of agreement.

At length White Buffalo's discourse came to an abrupt halt, and he looked down at Minny to translate. She was more than ready. 'White Buffalo speaks. His white brothers and the Great White Mother (Abbie), who has long looked after her Ute children, should listen, for he is going to tell of a big secret. The Ute people are today not as big as they were many moons ago. At that time they were so many that their tepees covered the land, and they traded with other tribes even as far as the great salt water

141

where the sun goes down in the evening.'

Abbie was mentally pleading with her friend just to get on with the story, but she knew that once Minny had a full head of vocal steam, she just had to tell the story her way.

Minny continued: 'The Ute people traded with the people that live by the great salt water (Pacific Ocean), but sometimes the path was blocked by enemies who said you must pay us so many buffalo hides to come this way. So the Ute people had to make another trail to keep away from the bad people. What he say, Abbie, is that there is another trail towards setting sun. A Ute secret, but he will show us the way and maybe we get ahead of Stoganoff.' (Minny never could wrap her tongue around that 'r' coming just after the 't'.)

Abbie was overjoyed with the thought that maybe they could get ahead of their adversary, but first of all she solemnly thanked White Buffalo for revealing this great secret, and received further information that the route would be difficult, especially with horses, but it was possible.

With White Buffalo leading the way, Abbie's party left the Old Spanish Trail and headed north in an ever-narrowing canyon that ascended steadily, suggesting that thousands of years ago it had probably been an active water course. That canyon led into another, where, for the most part, they were above the treeline; and then they entered a region where avalanches had thundered down, bringing not only snow but also tons of gravel and small rocks, which remained to litter and sometimes bury the trail after the sun had done its work. The trail changed direction and began to descend, and here they made their way along a ledge clinging to the side of a mountain, with a sheer face going up hundreds of feet on their left side while on their right was a yawning chasm, where, a thousand feet below, a carpet of pine trees waved gently like a green sea.

This was an area where the slightest misplaced step would spell disaster, and as the party made their way gingerly along, Abbie marvelled at the ancient Utes who had explored and pioneered this route to outwit their enemies. Finally, when they were several hundred feet lower and no fatalities had occurred, White Buffalo pointed ahead at a brown scar that appeared in the V of a canyon and traversed the valley below them, exclaiming excitedly to Minny words which she translated as, 'Lo! There is the Spanish Trail!'

CHAPTER 18

Relieved that they had survived their perilous detour without so much as a sprained ankle, Abbie's party thankfully made their way to a small cluster of habitations in the centre of the valley. The buildings turned out to be a livery stable, behind which was a large corral occupied by a number of shaggy ponies, proof of the skill of some wild horse hunter, a saloon combined with a general store bearing the slightly ridiculous title of 'The Mercantile Hotel', and two shacks, one of which had a sod-covered roof.

Arriving at the settlement, Abbie attended to the things common to any leader or commanding officer.

Horses were to be rubbed down and stabled with grain at the livery stable. Men were to be fed and arrangements made for their accommodation. Information was sought from the hotel owner, a certain Jose Miranda, regarding westbound traffic on the trail, and having determined that no party looking like any of Stroganoff's gang had put in an appearance, Abbie, having posted someone to watch the trail, could finally arrange for a room and time in the bath house, where she and Minny could remove some of the ravages of trail life.

Two hours later, with the exception of the one on guard, the whole group sat down to a hearty meal together, so different from the bolted food they had consumed hastily while on the Ute detour and indeed earlier. Just to sit at ease at a rough pine table and linger over country fried steak, bowls of creamy mashed potatoes, varied vegetables and rich sawmill gravy, washed down with copious mugs of hot black coffee, was luxury indeed, and Abbie revelled in this one chance to relax if only for a short while.

The meal concluded, the men filled their pipes, or extracted little sacks of Bull Durham tobacco from their vests and rolled their own cigarettes. They then proceeded to light up and enjoy the after-dinner companionship. Abbie looked at them all with true affection. These were her men, but it was never a mistress and servant situation. She knew that these men trusted her as she trusted them, and they would lay down their lives for each other. At the same time they would josh each other in that quiet western way, and include her in the circle of conversation, yet they never crossed the boundary of familiarity. The Utes during this time sat impassively, having eaten the food given to them with voracious appetites and drunk their coffee with suspicion, until they found that they could shovel into the hot steaming liquid as much sugar as they desired.

The pleasant interlude came to an abrupt end when a cry from Sam Brewer, posted as lookout on the porch of the hotel, warned that there was movement on the trail to the east. Alerted by Abbie not to make themselves conspicuous, the other men crowded to the window facing that direction, while Abbie, with her father's field telescope, knelt on the porch and, steadying the 'scope on the rail, brought the distant figures into focus.

A slight adjustment revealed the sorry condition of the approaching strangers. The first thing that struck Abbie was the poor condition of the mules, swaying with fatigue and obviously near the end of their tether. The mule handlers, most of whom were on foot, seemed to be in little better condition than their charges. The pedestrians were limping, and most were beating at the mules with switches to encourage them to increase the speed, while one was actually hanging on to the panniers of his particular animal as both staggered along. Of the three riders, two were slumped in the saddle obviously exhausted, while the third sat upright and seemingly alert as he brought up the rearguard of this column of the damned.

Abbie quickly devised a plan to force the oncoming men to surrender. 'Minny! You take White Buffalo and Young Deer through the back door of the hotel and circle round, hidden by that rise of ground, so that you can cover the trail from there!'

Minny nodded, and motioning to the two braves, they took their weapons and left as instructed. 'Sam, you and Johnny walk out casually and cross the trail talking to each other. Ignore the oncoming party and take a position in the livery stable. Keep under cover 'til I yell! Bill and Snowy . . .' this to the two remaining riders '. . . you remain with me. We are going to walk out on to the porch casually, as though just interested in the sight of newcomers. Those barrels at the east end of the porch should give us a bit of cover if any shooting starts, but I suspect that those men will surrender rather than fight. OK boys, let's get ready!' So saying, Abbie strolled out of the front door of the hotel, and shading her eyes with her left hand, took up a position leaning against the wall.

The exhausted mule train staggered to a halt in front of the hotel. Stroganoff's guttural voice ordered them to unpack the mules and to stack the boxes in a pile, while he would see to food and lodging. As he moved towards the steps leading up to the hotel porch, Abbie stepped forwards with her pistol drawn, halting the Russian's progress.

'Hold it right there, Count. I believe that you have my property in those boxes, and I think that now is the time to relieve you of it!' Abbie's party all brought their weapons into view to reinforce Abbie's demands – but Stroganoff's men, in a last sudden burst of energy, also pulled pistols and cocked aimed long guns at those in ambush.

The Russian, seeing Abbie hesitate to open fire against his wretched men, seized the opportunity and drew his own hand gun, a fierce-looking Lefaucheux Pinfire, similar to Abbie's pistol, but in 15mm calibre. She said later, that as her opponent's weapon swung in her direction, it was almost like staring into the entrance of the Thames tunnel.

Stroganoff broke the silence, 'So, young lady, I believe that we have reached an impasse, or what these Americans call, I believe, a Mexican stand-off! How do you propose that we end the situation? We both have our hammers cocked, and if one fired, even accidentally, the other would probably press the trigger in a reflex action. And no doubt, most of our respective followers are in a similar position.'

Abbie played for time, racking her brain in an attempt to discover a solution favourable to her side. She could not remain silent, and decided to work on the man's vanity. 'You know, Count, for a Russian you speak remarkably good English. Did you by any chance have an English tutor?'

Stroganoff literally smirked, as he loftily replied to Abbie's query, 'Young woman, if you had the slightest knowledge of aristocracy, you would realize that you are attempting to thwart one of the finest minds in Europe. Speaking English? Why, I can converse in any of half-a-dozen European languages other than your own barbaric tongue!'

Abbie's hands tightened on the grip of her pistol as the supercilious arrogance of the Russian noble confronting her struck home, and she responded tartly, 'Well, learning a language has not improved your qualities as a gentleman. You're still a common thief!'

A clatter of hoofs broke in on Stroganoff's intended reply, as a troop of United States cavalry coming from the western trail arrived in front of the hotel in a flurry of movement. Their commander, a bluff-looking officer with red nose and mutton-chop whiskers, introduced himself as Major Symon, and stated, 'All of you people on the porch, and all of you others hiding in that barn and other locations, holster your guns or face the consequences. This part of Utah Territory is now under martial law, and we will not permit any attempts to settle private disputes with gunfire while the Army is in command.'

Abbie, along with all the civilians present, both law keepers and law breakers, reluctantly holstered their pistols or lowered their rifles at the US major's order, as he turned, not to Abbie in her frontier garb of buckskin shirt and pants, but to the still elegantly attired gentleman with the distinguished features facing her. 'Now sir, what appears to be the problem here?'

In vain Abbie attempted to interject that she was the injured party in this dispute. The major raised one white gloved hand for her to be silent, indicating that she would get her chance to speak when he had heard what the 'gentleman' had to say. She had to stand there, with arms folded and inwardly boiling with rage, while Stroganoff in urbane tones described how this female scalawag and her gang had attempted to relieve him of all his goods and chattels.

The major, obviously swayed by the piteous story that he had just heard from Count Stroganoff, turned finally to Abbie and said severely: 'Now, young woman, what have you got to say for yourself before I formally arrest you and every one of your bunch of miscreants?'

Abbie took a deep breath and counted silently to fifty before she answered (there was obviously no point in an explosive retort with this hide-bound officer).

'Major, first of all allow me to introduce myself. My name is Lady Abigail Penraven, and I am a British subject. In many parts of the western United States I am commonly described as the Pinfire Lady. Furthermore, I have been sworn in as a special US deputy marshal by a representative of your Secretary of State, Mr Seward. I and my associates here have been pursuing this man and his gang for many days through Colorado Territory.' She would have continued, but the officer raised his hand for silence as, in the background, several of his men chuckled at some of the woman's manifestly ridiculous claims.

Ignoring the normal courtesies, Major Symon queried, 'Is there any way you can prove any of these preposterous claims?'

Abbie thought for a moment and then replied, 'Why yes Major! I believe I can. If you would accompany me to our room in the hotel. . . .' Major Symon stiffened visibly. 'Don't fret Sir! Your reputation is not in any danger. You may bring your sergeant if you wish, to vouch for the innocence of the visit. And perhaps leave a corporal's guard down here, maintaining that all is secure.'

The three went up to the room where Abbie and Minny had stowed their travelling traps, and the former took her saddle bags and emptied them on the small round table. 'You'll have to excuse the mess, Major. I'm afraid things aren't too tidy. We were not expecting an inspection.'

The major herumphed and coughed, scarlet in the face, as Abbie picked up and folded two pairs of lady's drawers as well as two cotton vests. Then she uncovered a large wallet and said, 'Aha! Let's see what we have in here,' and reaching in, she drew out a number of documents. Unfolding them one by one she stated the nature of each one as she passed them to Major Symon.

'Here is a Letter of Credit from my bank in England, stating that I can draw up to one hundred thousand pounds and the bank will cover it. Here is one of the Cunard tickets, the shipping line we used when returning to the United States. This is a receipt from Tipping and Lawden regarding repairs done in London to my Pinfire pistol, and here are sundry letters, bills and receipts that cover our land journey to Julesburg and south through Colorado Territory.

'Well Major? Are you now satisfied that I am who I told you I was?'

Major Symon, aware that he had made a fool of himself, nodded silently.

'Well, then, perhaps we may return to the hotel porch and prevent any gossip regarding your visit to a lady's bedroom. Sergeant, wipe that grin off your face, if you please.' This last remark was to the NCO, who was visibly amused by his commanding officer's discomfiture.

On the porch, Stroganoff, seated in a rocking chair, was becoming increasingly uncomfortable with the absence of his accuser, and initially was relieved when they returned. But his relief vanished when Major Symon declared that the lady – note, no longer 'woman' – had partially substantiated her story, and therefore no, he, Count Stroganoff, could not just depart as he desired.

Moments later his position was weakened still further by the arrival of a party of miners on their way to try their luck in California. 'Holy mackerel!' cried one of the newcomers, 'It's the Pinfire Lady! Hi, Lady Pinfire! I remember you at the shootout at Bailey's Ranch!' and he launched into a graphic account of what he had observed on that memorable occasion.

Stroganoff could see that his position was becoming increasingly shaky, and felt that it required him to adopt a reasonable air towards the situation. 'It would appear that we have somehow allowed a very simple problem to develop into an international incident. I'm sure that if we all just calm down and have a good night's rest, we will all see this situation in a different light in the morning.' He ended his proposal with a benign smile at all present.

Major Symon was intensely relieved at the Russian's reasonable suggestion, and it was agreed that all parties would meet at nine o'clock the following morning. Being the firstcomers, Abbie's group had laid claim to the hotel for their accommodation, so Stroganoff's men established a camp immediately to the east, and fortified with food purchased by their leader, settled down there for the night, while the cavalry made camp across the way beside the livery barn. With a military guard on all three groups, an uneasy night was passed by all.

Abbie had a restless night, as unable to sleep, she attempted to fathom what plans Stroganoff might be hatching to still attain his goal. She was relieved when a watery sun rose in the east to herald a new day.

After a satisfying breakfast, she and Minny repaired to the porch where it had been agreed that the meeting would take place. Shortly thereafter Major Symon, accompanied by his adjutant, marched smartly across the trail: he greeted Abbie courteously, nodded to Minny, and commandeered one of the rockers for his own use, while his companion stood leaning on the porch railing. And there they waited impatiently for the arrival of Count Stroganoff. Nine o'clock came and went, and still they waited.

Finally, Major Symon sent his orderly to enquire what was holding up the Russian's appearance. The orderly

returned and saluted, and reported: 'If you please, Sir, Lt
Schwartz says that the Count should be back any time now.
He told the lieutenant he was just taking two of his horses
out for a short run and would be back within the half
hour.'

'Congratulations, Major! I hope that you now realize
that by leaving Count Stroganoff at liberty you have probably placed the whole of the United States in danger. I'm
sure that the Secretary of State will be most interested to
learn how you mismanaged this affair!' And Abbie turned
away in disgust.

'Minny, dear! Would you please pick out our best two
horses. Saddle them, and I'll gather our traps together
and grab some supplies from the hotel. Sam!' This call was
to Sam Brewer, who was standing by awaiting Abbie's
orders. 'Sam, I'm leaving you in charge of our party here.
I'm quite sure that the major will willingly provide a guard
for the gold, and will cooperate with you until we return.
We have no time to lose!'

CHAPTER 19

Half an hour later, in possession of a military pass signed by Major Symon, Abbie and Minny with their selected horses were thundering westwards at a full gallop in pursuit of Count Stroganoff.

Abbie was unfamiliar with the trails over which they were passing, but was pretty sure that the Russian was no more at home in these parts. He would obviously keep as much as possible to the valleys and the lowland and thus avoid becoming lost amid the towering Rocky Mountains. The trail they were on was a well defined track, and the Count probably thought that he had a sufficient start on any likely pursuit so that, with two horses, he could outrun and thus lose his opposition.

The first day's ride was tiring and unfruitful, apart from a chance remark by one of several people Abbie spoke to during their chase. A travelling peddler mentioned that he had seen a man savagely beating a horse, but was vague as to the descriptions of either man or beast. Could that have been their quarry? There was no way of confirming the account, but Abbie thought it typical of Stroganoff's behaviour.

Nightfall found the two reluctantly making camp in a small grove of aspens off the main trail. Both girls would have liked to have ridden on through the night, but in totally unknown country that would have been a risky venture. So, after rubbing down their horses and hobbling them to prevent them straying, they settled down, as darkness fell upon the scene, to a scant meal of cold venison and sourdough biscuit, washed down with swigs of icy water from a rivulet trickling down from the heights above.

In the early morning both arose, stiff and cold, shivering in the misty dawn. Abbie suggested a warm cup of coffee to revive their spirits, to which Minny heartily agreed, and so, over a very small fire, they broke their fast; then shortly after performing scanty ablutions, they were on the trail once again.

Arriving at the little Mormon community of Beaver, they justified their journey to a rather officious young officer, who was the military representative in the village, and having declared with vigour that no, they were not seeking their husbands, Abbie finally extracted the information that Stroganoff had passed through the village the previous afternoon, and that both of his horses were badly lame.

They rode west, but shortly thereafter realized that because the trail was becoming increasingly impassable, the Russian could not have gone in that direction. They therefore retraced their route and followed a trail heading south towards Cedar City. Stroganoff must have also camped out the previous night, as in late morning a farmer, driving a heavily loaded wagon towards Beaver, vol-

unteered the information that an unsociable foreigner
had passed him riding south, mishandling two obviously
spent horses.

On the outskirts of Cedar City Minny spied a livery
stable with a large corral to the rear. 'Look Abbie! See in
corral, tired horses there!' Abbie looked in the direction
that Minny had indicated and saw the two black thor-
oughbreds standing there, heads down and flanks still
heaving, from the harsh usage to which they had been sub-
jected. Nobody had even bothered to remove the saddles
from the poor beasts, and Abbie and Minny took it upon
themselves to relieve the horses of this burden.

Leading their own steeds around to the front of the
livery stable, Abbie saw a small boy sitting on a bale of hay
and engrossed in a picture book, and called to him with a
smile, 'Tell me, are you the owner of this establishment,
young sir?'

The youngster looked up at the woman addressing him,
and quickly assured her that 'Ole Martin's the owner. But
I'm in charge when he's gone away,' he declared impor-
tantly. 'Whatja want?'

Abbie, a trifle irritated by the boy's ill manners, placed
one hand upon her pistol and demanded, 'I want some
good manners from you, young man, and I want some
information. There are two horses in a bad way in your
corral. Why are they left in that condition, and where is
the man who put them there?'

The stable boy, finding he was confronted by a lady
toting a large pistol, was impressed. She was obviously
someone to be reckoned with, so he shut his book and slid
down from his perch on the log. 'He's a stranger, Ma'am,

leastways, he ain't from around here. He comes in a little while ago. Puts the horses in the corral. Wouldn't let me unsaddle them, and gave me a measly dime to keep an eye on them.'

Abbie interrupted his flow of self-righteous indignation by raising a hand and inquired patiently, 'Tell me where the stranger went, please?' She produced a quarter and held it out to the stable boy.

'He asked me where he could get something to eat. I told him that folks say the best grub is to be found at the Bon Ton Café down there on the right, an' that's where he went, ma'am,' adding the salutation hopefully.

Abbie handed over the quarter, and then indicated that he could earn yet another quarter if he were to go down to the café and tell the stranger that a certain lady was waiting for him in the street. Turning to Minny, she asked her to walk around to the rear of the café, in case Stroganoff tried to make a hasty exit in that direction. Minny nodded, and slipping her Colt up and down in its holster significantly, hurried to do Abbie's bidding as the stable boy disappeared through the front door of the café.

Abbie waited under a tree across the road from the café. Would Stroganoff accept the challenge and face her, or would he once more try some other stratagem to avoid his well earned fate? During the time of waiting Abbie reflected on the many episodes in her life that had brought her to this situation, and pondered on her possible fate. Although confident of her gun-fighting skills and convinced of the justice she served, there was always the chance of failure. Was she to end her life pouring out her blood on to the dust of a Utah street, or would she prove to be triumphant?

While waiting, Abbie kept her eyes fixed on the front of the café, alert for any movement, and eventually was rewarded when a curtain was raised and then hurriedly lowered as someone within took a quick look at her location across the street. Abbie responded by moving to the other side of the tree, against which she had been leaning. Any change in position could disconcert a would-be opponent.

Finally, there was a movement at the door. It opened again half way, and the stable boy was thrust out and it closed again. The boy stumbled across the porch and jumping down, came running across the street. 'If you please, ma'am! That man inside the café said he's coming out but he ain't going to fight you. 'E says it ain't proper for a man to fight a lady. But I wouldn't trust 'im, ma'am. He wants his hosses ready for when he comes for them, but he still hasn't paid me!' He marched off down the street, a small figure full of injured pride.

The door opened once more and Count Stroganoff stood there motionless on the porch. He had removed the long Prince Albert coat that he habitually wore and carried it over his left arm. Abbie studied him carefully, from his black, high-crowned hat, his brocaded waistcoat – or 'vest', as Americans would call it – and his black trousers, much the worse for wear, stuffed into black riding boots badly in need of a good coat of polish. There was no sign of a holster or pistol.

He opened his arms wide, as though to verify that he was indeed unarmed, and stepped down from the porch with a broad smile on his face. By his gestures he obviously thought that Abbie would reciprocate by coming to meet him halfway, but she remained motionless and aloof in her stance.

Stroganoff had advanced about one third of the distance when Abbie spoke. 'That's far enough, Count! Do you intend to surrender to me? If so, put your coat down on the ground and raise your hands high above your head!'

The Russian did not reply, but nodded, and bent forward as though about to comply with Abbie's demand. But suddenly, his right hand dived beneath the coat he was carrying, where he had concealed his pistol, gripped by the barrel in his left hand. As his hand emerged, Abbie moved, taking a pace to the left and simultaneously doing her famous cross-draw, pulling her Pinfire pistol and cocking and firing it in one fluid motion. She cocked and fired again and again, each ball smashing into Stroganoff's brocaded vest. His one shot had smashed into the bark of the tree where Abbie had been standing. The count was driven back by Abbie's fire, his pistol flung wide as he fell on his back.

Abbie advanced with smoking pistol prepared to offer the coup de grâce, but there was no need: Count Stroganoff was dead, and so was his mad dream of Alaskiana.

There is not much more to tell to complete this story. Or is there?

Abbie and Minny returned to the ranch outside Colorado City, where they found that the stolen gold under a military escort had preceded them. Roger

Gotwald turned up to complete the story and tell how, upon arriving in San Francisco, he had enlisted the aid of the military unit at the Presidio and impounded a Peruvian barkentine which had been chartered by Hiram P. Markover and was found to contain as cargo two thousand rifles, powder and cast bullets.

Minny returned to her people, filling them with wonder of the things she had seen and done across the Great Water, and with a vow to Abbie that she would be available if ever her friend needed her again.

Gotwald brought with him an invitation for Abbie to visit Washington in the spring of 1867 as the guest of William Seward.

On 30 March 1867 the United States reached an agreement to purchase Alaska from Russia for a price of 7.2 million dollars.

A month later in a closed session of Congress, attended by Abbie, both House and Senate heartily endorsed a motion put forth by the right honourable William P. Seward that a certain Lady Abigail Penraven, otherwise known as the Pinfire Lady, be given honorary United States citizenship in consideration of her efforts to overcome the attempt to prevent the sale of Alaska.